THE DOG WHO
DARED TO DREAM

THE DOG WHO DARED TO DREAM

SUN-MI HWANG

Translated by Chi-Young Kim

Illustrations by Nomoco

ABACUS

ABACUS

First published in Great Britain in 2016 by Abacus

1 3 5 7 9 10 8 6 4 2

Copyright © Sun-mi Hwang, 2012

Translation copyright © Chi-Young Kim, 2016

The moral right of the author has been asserted.

Illustrations by Nomoco

Originally published in Korean as *Pureun gae jangbal* by
Woongjin Think Big Co., Ltd, South Korea, 2012

The Dog Who Dared to Dream is published with the support of
Literature Translation Institute of Korea (LTI Korea)

A CIP catalogue record for this book
is available from the British Library.

ISBN 978-0-349-14210-4

Printed and bound by CPI Group
(UK) Ltd, Croydon, CR0 4YY

Papers used by Abacus are from well-managed forests
and other responsible sources.

MIX
Paper from
responsible sources
FSC
www.fsc.org FSC® C104740

CONTENTS

THE OLD MAN

3

THE STRANGER

9

THE THIEF ON THE WALL

17

A SWEET FRIEND

27

SUSPICIOUS FOOD

37

HOMEWARD, ALONE

45

I'VE NEVER MET ANYONE LIKE YOU BEFORE

55

BETRAYAL

65

GRANDPA SCREECHER'S FOREARM

75

UNCERTAIN DAYS

83

KORI THE RASCAL
93

SISTER-IN-LAW
103

THOSE WHO ARE LEFT AND THOSE WHO LEAVE
111

THE COMING OF SORROW
123

WINDING STAIRCASE
135

FRIENDS
145

DIFFICULT WINTER
155

THE ROAD TO FRIENDSHIP
163

THE DOG WHO
DARED TO DREAM

THE OLD MAN

The brown dog lifted her head off the ground and growled as she nursed her pups. But that was it – she didn't even bare her teeth. 'I thought he'd come only after we starved to death,' she muttered.

The wire mesh gate, covered with a blanket, opened with a clang. Cold air rushed in. Shivering, she glimpsed the changing colours of the persimmon tree outside as the old man entered the large metal cage. His footsteps had given him away; she wouldn't have remained so calm if it had been anyone else. After all, it had only been thirteen days since she'd given birth.

The old man closed the gate behind him and placed a steaming pot on the ground. He blew out cigarette smoke, his face becoming blurry. 'Now you guys aren't so green any more,' he said, reaching down to remove the pups. They kept suckling, their eyes closed. 'You rascals! You'll kill her with all that sucking.'

'I'll say,' murmured the mother dog. She slowly got to her feet. 'This litter has quite an appetite.' She looked exhausted. Her teats were red and swollen and her fur was stiff. She began to wolf down her breakfast.

The old man crouched nearby and finished the rest of his cigarette, watching her. She was shivering. Her shoulder bones protruded from her thin frame. The pups snuffled around, looking for their mother's nipples, whining for her attention. She didn't pay them any mind, focused as she was on eating.

The man turned off the kerosene heater in the corner. It had been on all night long. 'All different colours,' he remarked.

Two were entirely brown, two were brown with white spots, three were brown with black spots, and one was very dark, almost bluish black.

'Just a few more days of hard work,' he said, stroking their mother with his rough hand. 'We'll find them owners soon.'

The mother dog finished the entire pot, but she wasn't quite full. She licked the remnants on the ground and looked up at the old man, who was holding a spotted puppy that had been pushed off the blanket they had been lying on.

He tutted. 'The firstborn ...' He looked down at it sadly. The puppy was already stiff. 'Weak from the very beginning, and now it's gone.'

'That one was born too weak,' sighed their mother. 'It didn't even suckle properly. Why is it always the firstborns that make me cry, every time?' She lay down again with a grunt. The pups burrowed into her, nudging her with their heads and tapping her with their front paws. Her belly jiggled gently. The babies struggled for nipples. The two strongest ones, both brown, pushed their siblings aside and settled in the middle. The black pup fell backwards in the tussle. She tried to push her way back in but couldn't clamber over her siblings' legs. Whimpering, she tried again. But nobody moved aside.

The old man gazed down at her. 'You're certainly not the weakest. Why are you letting yourself be shoved away?' He placed the small, lightweight pup on his palm. 'How did your mother come to have an odd one like you? Your fur's come in already. And you're all black!'

'It's a first for me, too,' said the mother dog. 'Their father doesn't look like that.'

The black pup sniffed the man's hand. It smelled of metal. She knew this scent. Earlier, her siblings had pushed her, causing her to topple over onto the bare floor. She had hit her head on the wire mesh, and this smell had enveloped her. Her eyelids fluttered, her head hurting anew. She opened her eyes slowly to see the man's wrinkled face, patchy with dark scabs, burned by the sparks that landed on his face when he soldered.

'Look at you! You're the first to open your eyes!' The old man plucked a brown pup nestled in the middle and set down the blue-black puppy in its place.

THE STRANGER

'**P**ut him down at once!' Grandpa Screecher swung the broom.

Startled, the mother dog dropped Spot, who was whining pitifully. Barking, the mother fled to the vegetable garden where the cabbage for the winter kimchi was almost ready to pick.

'Bad dog!' screamed Grandpa Screecher, waving the broom. 'Come out of there right this instant!'

The puppies called the old man Grandpa Screecher because he shouted and yelled so much. But it was partly the pups' fault. They roamed as a pack and destroyed things, chewing up shoes, playing with the tray Grandma left on top of the earthenware pots in the yard, eating all the fish drying on a tray, gnawing on slices of dried courgette. When they grew bored of chewing on the vegetables, they pooped on them. They swatted at clean washing that had fallen on the ground. Once, they even managed to get into the shed and played with a cord, which ended up winding itself around one pup's neck and nearly suffocating him.

'Where's my eldest?' barked their mother from the vegetable patch. 'Where is she?'

Of course, Grandpa Screecher couldn't understand what she was saying. 'Now you're really getting on my nerves!' he shouted, running over with the broom in his hand. She hid behind the earthenware pots then ran into the yard. She scurried back into the vegetable patch and then into the shed. All the while, she kept barking, 'Where's my eldest? Where is she?'

Scraggly, the black puppy, crouched under the window and watched her mother and Grandpa Screecher running around. She could tell her mother was incensed. She would have to take care not to get bitten like poor Spot. Her mother had been angry a few days ago, too. A stranger had walked straight into their cage, stepping on their blanket. He smelled unfamiliar. Then, he had taken one of her spotted siblings.

The same thing had happened this morning. A man came to see Grandpa Screecher, then took the eldest home with him. But their mother had gone out to the poultry farm with Grandma and had missed the transaction. Scraggly didn't like how the man smelled – scorched. He was wearing shoes that had been burnt. When the stranger came closer to her, grinning, Scraggly curled into herself. She would bite him if he even dared to reach towards her. But he didn't so much as glance at her.

'Nice antics!' A hair-raising chortle came from the top of the wall to interrupt Scraggly's thoughts. It was the old cat.

Scraggly glared at the cat, who was perched high up. Scraggly didn't trust the old beast. All she did was creep around silently, spying on everyone. Scraggly barked. The cat sneered, her eyes narrowing and her sharp teeth flashing. Scraggly felt the hair on her back rise. The old cat laughed, pacing slowly along the top of the neighbour's wall, making Scraggly feel dizzy. The man who had taken the eldest had spoken in a hoarse voice, just like the cat. She barked at the cat, who swiped at her then disappeared down the other side of the wall.

'Stop it, both of you,' grumbled Grandma as she came out of the kitchen. 'Dog and man – you're as bad as each other!'

'What did you say?' Grandpa Screecher shouted in indignation. 'Dog and man?'

Grandma pretended not to hear. She placed an apron and a straw coil in a big basin, preparing to go to the market to sell fish. She went to work in the morning and came back after dark with leftover fish parts, which she boiled for the dogs' food. The puppies always wagged their tails when they heard her approach for this very reason. 'You need to put the money from selling the puppies in the bank,' she reminded Grandpa. 'Chanu will be sending Dongi to nursery school soon. I'd like us to give them a little something. As his grandparents.' With that, she placed the basin on her head and left the house.

'Money for Dongi's nursery school?' complained Grandpa Screecher. 'What has Chanu done for us? How are we supposed to afford that? I'm behind on the rent at the shop and I have to pay for the bicycle parts I brought in.' He leaned the broom against the persimmon tree and filled a bucket of water at the tap. He lugged it into the cage as the puppies scampered behind him, sticking their snouts in the bucket. Their mother joined them.

Awkwardly Scraggly got to her feet but watched from afar. Her mother would push her away if she tried to join in. Scraggly fought back when it was her siblings who pushed her aside, but she knew it was better to keep her distance with her mother, who didn't seem to like her. 'She a bit scruffy, that one,' her mother would mutter audibly.

Whenever she heard her mother grumbling, Scraggly looked down at her feet. It was because of her fur, all black and shaggy, flopping over her eyes. At certain angles, it even looked blue. Her siblings treated her poorly, following their mother's lead. They didn't allow her to come near them; they didn't like to share their food. So Scraggly learned to snatch her portion and gulp it down.

Grandpa Screecher let out a long whistle. 'Scraag! Come on.'

She trotted over and pushed her snout in the bucket, lapping water. When Grandpa Screecher was there, her mother didn't bother her much. She was glad he was there; if her siblings happened to kick the bucket over while frolicking, she wouldn't have another chance to drink anything until Grandma and Grandpa returned home for the night.

Grandpa Screecher stroked her back. 'You odd dog,' he murmured. 'Who will you go to?' She shrank but didn't flee; his hand was rough, but it was warm. Grandpa Screecher sometimes called her 'Scraag!' Her long shiny black fur got curlier the longer it grew. She looked very different from her brothers and sisters, but she was the only one Grandpa Screecher named.

THE THIEF ON THE WALL

It had been cold the night before. Everything was frosted white; the wall, the branches, the cabbage in the vegetable patch, the straw piled up in the rice paddies in front of the house. The frost gradually melted under the morning sun. A magpie flew up to the top of the tree to peck at the persimmons. It sounded an alarm when it spotted the old cat ambling along the top of the wall.

'Have you sold that bicycle you built?' asked Grandma as she heaved the basin onto her head to go to work.

Grandpa Screecher rubbed the frost off his bicycle seat with a towel. 'I fixed a few leaky tyres. If I could sell the bicycles I built, we'd be rich by now. If someone wants them, I'm just going to give them a good price.'

'Well don't give them too big a discount,' Grandma advised. 'You've worked so hard on those bikes. You were staring at them for days! Don't be so easily swayed. Don't give them away just because someone says nice things.'

'Me? Easily swayed?' Grandpa Screecher's voice climbed.

Grandma walked out of the gate. 'They put out rat poison because of the fallen harvest grain,' she reminded him. 'Make sure this gate is secure before you leave. We don't want the dogs to get out and fall ill.'

'What am I, their father?' Grandpa Screecher flicked his towel and grumbled, but Grandma was already out of earshot. He looked at the cage. The puppies had been watching, their heads poking out. They squirmed back in when they met his eyes.

'Rat poison, that's dangerous.' Grandpa Screecher picked up two wood planks, which were standing next to the cage. 'I'll make sure they're safe. They'll bring me a tidy sum, after all.' He glanced at the gate, his frown softening. 'Going out to sell fish when she's feeling unwell ... poor thing. And we have a son and a daughter who should help.' He placed the planks on the back of his bicycle.

The puppies poked their heads out of the wire mesh door, which was open. Their mother was in her kennel, positioned next to the cage, dozing with her head on her front legs.

Grandpa Screecher tapped the wire cage. 'Stay awake and guard the house! I can't keep you cooped up in that cage all day, but don't get out of that gate.'

The mother dog startled awake and stood. The puppies lowered their tails and retreated into the corner. Grandpa tied the mother dog up, which is what he did each time he left the house – he had to ensure his prime breeder was safe. 'Grandma went to work even though she's ill,' he addressed the dogs bitterly, as though it were their fault that Grandma couldn't rest. 'You guys take good care of the house, got it?'

The mother dog was unfazed. 'Goodness, my ears.'

Goldie, the big brown pup, mimicked her. 'Goodness, my ears.'

Their mother snapped, 'Watch your manners!'

Goldie whimpered and the others cowered.

Grandpa Screecher laughed. 'No need to be so harsh to your babies,' he said. 'There's no point. I was like that, and look where it's got me. They think they raised themselves! They don't want to live with you, and they don't even pick up the phone when their mother is ill.' He wheeled his bicycle to the gate.

The dogs wagged their tails goodbye.

Grandpa Screecher went outside and stood the planks up against the gate, blocking the gap underneath, just to be safe.

Scraggly stayed close to the gate, her ears pricked until she heard the bicycle wheels turning. She wanted to go along. She went under the persimmon tree and licked a fruit that had splattered when the magpie dropped it. It was slightly frozen and cool on her tongue.

'I'm hungry, too,' said an unpleasant voice from above her.

Scraggly looked up. The old cat was pacing along the top of the wall, giving off an unsavoury smell. Scraggly looked for her mother, but she was already halfway inside her kennel, dozing again, and her siblings were tumbling around the vegetable garden, playing a vigorous game of hide-and-seek.

'They put poison traps all over the paddies,' said the cat, grinning. 'Same thing every time they harvest. So stupid! Now I won't be able to eat rats for a few days. Don't you feel bad for poor old me?' The cat crouched low on the wall.

Scraggly flinched, half expecting the cat to leap off the wall and land in the yard.

'You must be bored,' the cat continued insincerely. 'Want me to play with you?'

Scraggly barked loudly enough for her mother to hear. Her mother woke and growled. The puppies began barking from the vegetable garden.

'Suit yourself,' the cat hissed. She leaped off the wall into her own yard.

Scraggly kept barking.

'Shush!' scolded her mother. 'I'm trying to sleep.'

Scraggly grew quiet, but the smell of the cat lingered and bothered her. She began to poke around under the persimmon tree. She heard a commotion from the vegetable patch; the others were ganging up on Baby. The black spotted pup was the smallest and weakest. Scraggly went closer. 'Stop that, all of you!' she called.

'Get lost,' snapped Goldie.

Baby was licking his leg, whimpering. Was his leg bleeding?

'You bother me again and I'm going to bite you on the other leg!' warned Goldie before stalking out of the vegetable garden. The others followed, and Baby remained where he was, crying and licking his leg. It wasn't the first time Goldie had pushed the others around, taking advantage of her size.

Scraggly gave up and went off to find something to do. She found a wooden box under the persimmon tree. Settling down, she began to gnaw on it, giving relief to her emerging teeth. All of them liked to chew on this, like the wire mesh, but Goldie preferred shoes, which got her into plenty of trouble with Grandpa Screecher. After a while, Scraggly noticed music coming from far away. Once, her mother had told her it was coming from a church; she had been heading towards it when she met their father.

Goldie was now gnawing on clean washing scattered by the wind and the spotted pups were grooming each other's faces. Their mother was in a deep sleep. The day was quiet and warm sunlight filled the yard.

Suddenly, a scream pierced the air. Everyone turned to look at the vegetable garden. The old cat slipped out between the cabbages and leaped onto the wall.

'What happened?' Their mother pulled at her chain but she couldn't get free.

Scraggly bounded into the vegetable garden. She had recognised it as Baby's scream. She was closely followed by her siblings. They found Baby lying in a furrow. 'Get up,' Scraggly said, licking his face. But Baby opened his eyes weakly and just looked at her. Scraggly's nose wrinkled involuntarily; her sibling smelled like the old cat. He was bleeding from the neck. It was a deep wound.

'Mum! Mum!'

'Baby is hurt!'

'The cat did it!'

The puppies burst into tears. Their mother strained at the chain, barking. She could do nothing but leap up and run around her kennel. 'Lick him!' she called. 'Bring him here.'

But none of them could take care of him like she could. They began to fret. 'He can't get up!'

'Mum, you have to come!'

'Baby, come here!' their mother called, yanking and tugging the chain. Her tongue hung out and she panted. Every time she leaped up, the metal chain clanked and the kennel shuddered. But she couldn't move it, as it was bolted to the ground.

Baby panted in distress, groaning. Tears streamed down his face. Finally, his eyes closed. He stopped moving.

Their mother looked up at the sky and howled in sorrow.

Scraggly glanced up at the top of the wall, her eyes filled with tears. The old cat was curled up nonchalantly, licking her lips with her long tongue.

'You're wicked!' Scraggly shouted.

'Why is it my fault?' the cat asked lazily. 'I didn't decide to get hurt and start giving off a nasty smell.' Slowly she got to her feet and walked back and forth along the top of the wall. She seemed poised to do something else to Baby. Her stripes were making Scraggly dizzy.

Their mother howled again. Church music spread gently throughout the village. That evening was a sad one; after Baby was buried under the persimmon tree, a nearby resident came by and took a spotted pup with her.

A SWEET FRIEND

Snow had fallen overnight. Scraggly woke early and scampered around, making paw prints on the snow. It tickled the bottom of her feet and she couldn't walk straight. Giggling, she roamed the snow-covered vegetable garden. A magpie sang in the barren persimmon tree, its song ringing out clear and high. It flew down and settled in front of the kennel. It pecked at the empty dog bowl. It looked around dejectedly before flying back up to the tree.

The window flew open. Grandpa Screecher's lined face peeked out along with that of a child. It was his grandson, Dongi, who had arrived late the previous night.

'Wow, look! Snow!' Dongi clapped.

'And a lot of it.' Grandpa Screecher clapped as well.

Dongi rushed outside, startling Goldie, who was crouched in front of the door, playing with a small shoe she had pulled out from under it.

'Hey, that's mine!' Dongi cried.

The top of the shoe looked chewed. Even though Goldie had moved away from the door, the shoe remained in her mouth.

'My shoe.' Dongi's lip trembled.

Goldie approached, wagging her tail.

Dongi's face turned red. He dropped onto the ground and burst into tears. Goldie bounced up and down, placing her paws playfully on Dongi's chest.

'How could you do that?' screamed Dongi, his small fists balled. He slapped Goldie, who whimpered and flattened herself on the ground.

Scraggly and Spot paused their frolicking. 'I knew this would happen! Serves you right!' said Spot triumphantly, laughing. Goldie had never been swatted. But Goldie glared at him, so Spot turned his attention to gnawing on the chain-link cage. Scraggly approached Goldie cautiously. She wanted to help her; if she had licked Baby more and managed to comfort him, he may not have had to die.

'Give it back!' screamed Dongi, stomping his little feet. 'Give it back!'

The adults rushed out at the commotion. Grandpa Screecher was first, followed by Dongi's mum. Grandma came out of the kitchen, ladle in hand, and Dongi's dad, Chanu, walked out, looking groggy.

Grandpa discovered the ragged shoe and turned to fix the pups with a glare. 'You rascals.' He stepped into the yard and picked up the broom.

Goldie lowered her tail and slunk backwards.

'Run!' Scraggly stamped her front paws.

Goldie sped off, with Grandpa Screecher chasing her, swinging the broom. Goldie ran by the earthenware pots and galloped down to the vegetable garden, then squirmed under the gate and fled outside.

Enraged, Grandpa Screecher returned, his breath visible in the air. He suddenly swiped at Scraggly. 'How could you ruin brand new shoes like that?' The broom scratched Scraggly.

Scraggly ran off. It was so unfair. After all, she hadn't done a thing. She looked back, feeling sad. Grandpa Screecher was still brandishing the broom.

'Grandpa,' Dongi managed, sniffling, 'it was Goldie.'

Grandpa Screecher didn't apologise to Scraggly. Instead, he began to sweep the snow in the yard. 'Where did that mutt learn to chew on shoes?' he grumbled.

Scraggly's back stung. She lowered her head and went inside her cage. It didn't make sense. Sometimes Grandpa Screecher seemed to cherish her, but other times he treated her like an outcast. She wouldn't go near him when he yelled at her like that.

After breakfast, Grandpa Screecher went out to buy Dongi new shoes. But he came back quickly; the shop was closed for New Year's.

'How can you eat after destroying Dongi's new shoes?' Grandpa Screecher complained to Goldie, who was gulping down rice-cake soup. But Goldie didn't stop – she never relented when it came to food.

Their mother chewed happily on a bone, a rare treat. 'Puppies are like that,' she mumbled. 'They make mistakes before they learn. We have to sharpen our teeth. It's what we've done for generations.'

Scraggly finished eating and lay in the sun. Spot tried to get her to play but feeling morose, she wouldn't budge. Dongi came over, his tiny feet encased in his grandfather's big fur-lined shoes. Scraggly tensed but didn't move away.

'You're like a lion,' Dongi said, squatting next to her. She stared at the little boy, at his twinkling eyes and his ruddy cheeks. 'Your hair is so long. Way too long.' He patted her head, stroked her back, poked her leg, and pushed the overgrown hair out of the way to look into her eyes. He smelled sweet. The boy rummaged in his pocket and took something out. 'Here. It's chocolate.'

Scraggly sniffed the small round thing. She ate it. She had never tasted this before, but it was delicious. She licked Dongi's palms again and again.

'That tickles! You're tickling me!'

Scraggly liked the giggling Dongi. She liked his sweet voice, so unlike Grandpa Screecher's. His small hand was gentle and kind. Dongi brought a comb and groomed Scraggly's long fur. He gathered the hair covering her eyes and fastened it to the side with a clothes peg. It tickled but felt exhilarating all the same. Scraggly closed her eyes and relaxed.

'I want to be groomed, too!' Spot said, bouncing around them.

'Me too, me too! Better me than her, she's dirty.' Goldie was envious.

'Yeah, and she's also a loner.'

They rolled and jumped around, but Dongi was having fun with Scraggly's long hair and didn't even look at the other puppies.

'Dongi, let's go home.' Chanu lifted him up, since he didn't have any shoes to go home in.

Dongi's mother stepped out with several bags in each hand. Scraggly cocked her head. Hadn't she only brought one bag when they arrived?

Grandpa Screecher's face was sullen. 'Why leave so soon? All you had time to do was ruin your nice new shoes. You could wait until we buy him a new pair tomorrow.'

Scraggly wondered if anyone had heard him. Dongi's parents continued towards the gates, and Grandma followed, carrying more things for them. Grandpa grudgingly followed but stopped at the gate.

'Goodbye,' Dongi's mother said. 'We'll be back soon.'

Chanu walked out of the gates without a word. Dongi waved from his father's arms. 'Bye, Scraggly!'

Scraggly tagged along. She wished they would stay. She wanted to play with Dongi. She paced between Chanu and Grandpa Screecher, but soon had to stop. Dongi and Chanu were already so far away.

'So many things in life don't go the way you want,' Grandpa Screecher mumbled to himself, sighing. 'Chanu won't keep ignoring us when he's a bit more successful, I'm sure of it. He'll ask us to come and live with him. It's silly to want something when we haven't been able to do anything for them.' His shoulders slumped. 'The house is going to feel empty. They don't come as often as they should . . . I'm going to miss the boy.' He picked up the broom and began to sweep the yard, even though there was no longer any snow to clear.

The mother dog tensed and began barking. A few moments later, their neighbour stepped in through the gates. 'What are you doing?' she asked playfully. 'Are you trying to make your yard all spotless?'

Grandpa leaned the broom against the persimmon tree, looking bashful.

Scraggly went over to sniff the neighbour's leg. She smelled of the earthy Chinese medicine she used in her acupuncture practice.

The acupuncturist examined Goldie. 'Sell me that one,' she offered. 'I'll make it worth your while.'

Goldie pricked up her ears and barked. Spot followed suit. Their mother was the loudest among them all. Scraggly felt panicked. Sell? That meant Goldie would leave home and never return.

'No, not that one.' Grandpa shook his head.

Scraggly looked at Goldie in surprise. Grandpa Screecher scolded Goldie all the time. Did he like her after all? Who would he sell, then? Scraggly's hair stood on end.

'Oh, are you raising her to be the breeder?'

'Of course. She's the strongest of them all.'

'I like her best, though. I'm only interested in her.' The acupuncturist tried again.

'Sorry, not that one. The mother is too old to breed now.' Grandpa Screecher looked at Spot and then at Scraggly. Scraggly shrank away, afraid that she would be offered up for sale. She turned and walked slowly into the cage.

SUSPICIOUS FOOD

'The young grow up and the old become exhausted. Only if you live through winter do you understand what it's hiding. Winter has many secrets,' said the old cat from the top of the wall. These days, she moved slower and her voice was weaker. She was thin; perhaps winter had been harsh to her.

'Don't you even think about coming this way,' snapped Scraggly.

Though safely seated on the wall, the old cat flinched. The puppies had grown quite a bit. 'Winter's done something to you, too,' she hissed, her eyes narrowed to slits.

'Done something to me?'

'Look at yourself. You've changed. I've never seen a dog like you.'

Scraggly didn't like how the old cat was cocking her head. What could winter have done to her? Her mother hadn't said anything. Then again, she never did like Scraggly to come near her.

'Hey,' called the old cat to their mother. 'Who's Scraggly's father?'

'How dare you? What are you insinuating?' Their mother glared at the cat.

The old cat snickered. 'I always thought it was odd that this one is blue-black and hairy. And now she's sprouting white hair! Is she ageing even when she's not grown up yet? The curse of winter has got to her.'

White hair? Scraggly examined herself. Her long, wiry hair was covered in what looked like dust. She had thought it was because she roamed the streets. Was that not it?

'I'm certain that winter has done something to you,' said the cat.

'What has it done?' Scraggly asked.

The cat tutted. 'Silly dog! You want me to spell it out?'

'Why don't you tell me? I'm sure it will be rubbish,' Scraggly shot back.

'How rude! You dogs look down at the ground all day and can't do anything about it. You can't see the bigger picture.'

'Shut up and get lost!' growled their mother.

The old cat sauntered down to the end of the wall. She yawned, curled her back, and stretched. Her teeth were still sharp and she looked limber. 'Don't be grouchy. It's obvious that winter has it in for you and she won't stop there. Now your master's fallen ill and he's had to go to hospital first thing this morning. I know what's going on in the neighbourhood from my perch up here.'

'Shut up!' Their mother leaped to her feet, but the chain held her back with a clang.

A voice called from the other side of the wall. 'Kitty, time for food!'

'Indeed it is,' the old cat said, and disappeared with a grin.

Scraggly lay down under Grandpa Screecher's bicycle. The cat's words had bothered her. What was winter doing to her? She examined her front paws. Different-coloured hair was mixed in with the black. When had this happened? She licked it all but it tasted the same. She decided to go to her mother. 'Mum, what happened to me?'

Her mother didn't open her eyes. 'Don't worry about it.'

'I think I have changed. What has winter done to me?'

'Don't you worry about what that alley cat said. You're just you. Nothing's changed.'

'My hair ... '

Her mother frowned.

Scraggly paused.

'Well, you're that way because we have many ancestors,' her mother finally said.

'Ancestors?' Scraggly cocked her head.

Her mother coughed. 'Many ancestors make many descendants. You don't understand yet. I think you look like our *sapsal* ancestors.'

'So their fur—'

'Foolish child!' snapped her mother. 'Grandpa Screecher's in the hospital. When the owner is not well, the family is supposed to wait quietly. That's our duty.' She closed her eyes again.

Her mother had never given her so many answers before. Scraggly knew she couldn't continue asking. Crestfallen, she crept back under the bicycle.

Grandpa Screecher had been very ill for several days. Grandma stayed home and took care of him, and the dogs were given only rice for their meals. Grandpa Screecher didn't sweep the yard in the mornings and the bicycle stayed put. He didn't work in the flowerbed or in the vegetable garden, which remained only partially tilled.

A *sapsal* dog. But her hair hadn't been like this before. She recalled Grandpa Screecher mentioning that he didn't feel as good as before. And then he had fallen ill. Scraggly looked up at Dongi's trousers hanging on the clothesline. The little boy had visited a few days before. Grandpa Screecher's son and daughter came with their families to visit their ill father. Dongi played only with Scraggly, splashing water and running through the yard and the vegetable garden. He would have continued playing if his mum hadn't come out to scold him about getting his trousers wet. When he went home, Dongi wore the new red shoes Grandpa Screecher had bought. After Grandpa Screecher brought them back to the house, he had placed them on top of the shoe cabinet in case Goldie decided to chew on the replacements. Grandpa Screecher had hummed, one shoe in each hand, dancing about as though he were holding the boy himself. When Grandma walked in, he had stopped immediately and pretended that he had been doing something else.

'I'm hungry,' grumbled Spot. 'Where is everyone?'

'I'm starving! We haven't eaten all day!' Goldie licked the empty bowl. Even the water bowl was empty.

'Mum, when's Grandma coming back?' whined Spot.

Their mother didn't open her eyes, dozing as always. Had winter done something to her, too? Scraggly wandered over to the gate, perplexed. She smelled something. She vaguely remembered this scent. Her ears pricked up. She stuck her nose out through the gap in the gate and sniffed.

It was stronger. She heard the whirr of a bicycle. Scraggly looked behind her at the bicycle standing in the yard. It wasn't Grandpa Screecher's.

Goldie sensed it too. Spot came over as well, listening attentively. 'Food!' Goldie cried.

Spot barked. Their mother opened her eyes and stood up slowly.

Scraggly's head began to pound. Her chest grew tight. She had heard this sound before; an unfamiliar bicycle passing in front of the gate. She barked at it each time, but now something was different.

The bicycle stopped outside. Scraggly heard steps – unfamiliar footsteps. The smell grew stronger. 'What is this? It smells terrible!' Scraggly paced back and forth, growing concerned.

Spot and Goldie sniffed the air, uneasy. Their mother licked her chops and pulled at her chain, causing it to bang against her kennel and rattle. The smell and steps continued to approach; Scraggly paced faster and Spot and Goldie began leaping about. Their mother kept pulling. Amidst the unfamiliar smell was the scent of food.

Something flew over the wall and landed precisely in front of their mother's kennel. It was a chunk of meat.

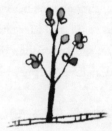

HOMEWARD, ALONE

Scraggly sniffed the meat and stepped back. 'This doesn't smell right.' But her mouth was watering already. She almost lunged at it but caught herself. She had smelled this odd whiff before. It made her head throb and her fur stand on end.

Their mother growled and smelled the meat. Spot and Goldie ran around their mother, but didn't dare sneak a bite. 'It does smell a bit, doesn't it?' Their mother sniffed and poked at the meat. 'Is it rotten?' Spot and Goldie crowded her. Their mother glared at them to keep them at bay.

'Mum, we're hungry!' whined Spot.

'I want it now! I'm hungry!' Goldie moaned.

They were all very hungry, on the verge of collapsing. They hadn't even had a sip of water since Grandpa Screecher and Grandma had rushed out that morning.

'I know, I know. We're in no position to be picky.' Their mother took a bite.

'Mum, no!' Scraggly stamped her feet and barked.

Her mother ignored her and tore at the meat.

Scraggly gulped. She was so hungry that her stomach was twisted in knots.

'I want some!' Spot and Goldie grabbed the meat at opposite ends and pulled, growling. Scraggly paced around them anxiously. She was so hungry that she was drooling, but the unpleasant stink was making her head hurt.

Her family ate up the meat without leaving any behind. Still hungry, they sniffed along the ground.

Scraggly sniffed with them, still drooling. She should have had a bite. Everyone was fine, after all. Scraggly's stomach growled. If only she had taken one bite! She felt low, watching her family bouncing around with newfound energy. Her suspicions had been unwarranted; now she wouldn't get to eat anything. She felt dizzy. She went back to the bicycle and curled up beneath it. She should have just taken a bite. Scraggly swallowed the saliva that had pooled in her mouth and closed her eyes. She might as well sleep. Hopefully it would be dark when she woke up and Grandma would be back. Maybe she would give them bean-paste soup and rice. She shook her head. She shouldn't think about food; she should just try to sleep.

The gate creaked open.

Scraggly raised her head in surprise.

A man was stepping inside, wheeling a large bicycle. But it wasn't Grandpa Screecher.

'Who are you?' barked Scraggly. 'Mum! It's a stranger!'

Nobody moved. Nobody raised their heads or made a sound. Something bad had happened. Scraggly ran to her mother and nudged her. But she didn't stir. They were all sleeping as soundly as though it were the middle of the night. They were even snoring. Scraggly backed away, barking at the top of her lungs.

'That one didn't eat it?' grumbled the stranger.

That voice! Scraggly barked again, the hair on her neck bristling. It brought to mind an old shoe, scorched by fire. That smell had given her a headache when her spotted sibling was taken. Grandpa Screecher had been there that day, though. What was this man doing here right now?

'Get out!' Scraggly barked. 'Nobody's home!'

'Damn. I'm not going to be able to take her quietly,' the interloper muttered to himself. He propped his bicycle up and glanced at Scraggly as he lifted up a small wire cage from the back of the bike.

Scraggly barked and barked. She leaped about, making a ruckus, but the stranger wasn't cowed. He opened his cage and lifted her mother inside. Her mother was limp.

'Stop that! What are you doing?' Scraggly yelled.

'Too thin and too old. She's not going to be worth it. I hope I get a good price for the puppies, at least.' The stranger moved deliberately, as if he had known nobody would be home. He picked Goldie up and put her in the cage.

Barking, Scraggly sprang forward and bit his forearm.

'Ow! You little—' The man smacked her on the head.

She fell back, but she leaped up and lunged at him again.

The man picked up the chain her mother had been wearing. 'You're quite something! You really must have some ferocious *sapsal* blood in you. All right, you're definitely coming with me.'

Scraggly barked and barked. She wished Grandpa Screecher would hurry back. The stranger shook the chain to keep Scraggly away and grabbed Spot by the neck. He dragged him along. Her brother's body was slack. He looked pitiful.

Scraggly leaped at him again, but the man was faster. He kicked her and she fell to the side. Now her entire family was shut in the small cage.

'Mum! Wake up!' screamed Scraggly. 'Open your eyes!'

The man approached her, the chain dragging on the ground. The rattling sound struck her heart. Her body burned up and her head pounded.

'Come, puppy. Good dog.' The stranger grinned. His teeth were yellow.

Scraggly lowered her body, signalling defeat, but then shot forward. She bit him on the ankle and held on. The man screamed and fell on his behind. He hit her again. Her head felt like it would explode. She refused to let go. The man pried her jaw open with both hands.

A sound came from next door.

Scraggly tumbled across the yard. Blood trickled down her face. Trembling, she stood and glared at the man.

'This is ridiculous.' The man got up and limped to his bicycle.

Scraggly sprang forward, but the world spun and she collapsed.

She got to her feet, woozy, but the man was wheeling his bicycle out.

'No!' She burst into tears and ran after him.

He was already on his bicycle and speeding down the narrow alley along the fences. She ran after him, panicked. She forgot about her headache and the blood on her face.

'Stop, thief! Let them go!' She sprinted after him.

The bicycle was so fast that she couldn't catch up. She ran down the narrow alley and crossed the street. Her heart was in her throat. Her chest felt tight. She managed to catch up to the bicycle wheels on the hill by the embankment.

'Whoa, you little—' The bicycle wove.

Running alongside, Scraggly sank her teeth into the man's foot. He tried to shake her off but she held on tight. The bicycle wobbled but kept going. The stranger's shoe slipped off. Thinking it was his foot, she tore at it, but suddenly her side erupted in pain. He had kicked her again.

'You piece of shit!'

Scraggly whimpered and fell off the embankment into the creek with a splash. The water was cold; snow had fallen earlier in the morning. Scraggly splashed and trod water. She was frozen to the bone and her body felt stiff. 'Help!' She paddled with all her might until she reached dry ground. She rested her head on a pile of dried waterweed and closed her eyes for a while. Her teeth chattered. The man and his bicycle were no longer in sight. Only the darkness and cold wind surrounded her. She waddled up to the road and shook off the water, but she was soaked through. The breeze stung her skin.

She spotted the old shoe she'd yanked off the man's foot. Shivering, she wailed, 'How could this have happened?' There was nothing she could do here; she had to go home. She held the shoe in her mouth and turned around. Perhaps everyone would make it back somehow. If her mother had woken up in the cage, she would have been incensed. She was terrifying when she was angry; there was no way she would let the crook take everyone like that. Scraggly padded home. Icicles started to form in her long hair as she walked, her tail drooping. This must have been it; this terrible development must be what winter really had in store for her. Why would winter do this to her? Did winter hate her? Scraggly turned down the alley and arrived at the narrow path along the wall. She walked slowly, lifting her head to look at the end of the alley. She couldn't hear anyone. Her throat closed up. Hot tears flowed from her eyes.

Then, she spotted Grandpa Screecher, standing like a shadow in front of the gate. She let out a whimper with the old shoe still clenched between her teeth.

'Scraag?' Grandpa Screecher's voice was shaking.

She limped up to him. He bent down and opened his arms, and she fell into them in a heap.

'What's this?' He squinted and pried her mouth open. He stared at the old shoe, his face crumpling in anger. He looked at Scraggly, her frozen fur, and the old shoe. He gently embraced her. A deep moan escaped from his trembling embrace.

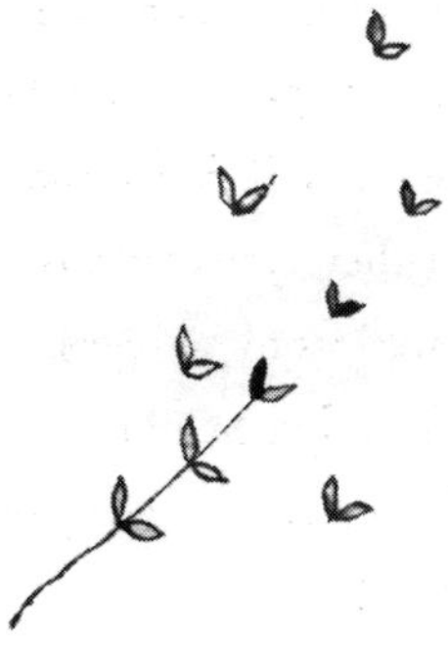

I'VE NEVER MET ANYONE LIKE YOU BEFORE

'Don't go wandering about,' Grandpa Screecher admonished, though by now Scraggly was fully grown. Nevertheless, his nagging had increased markedly. Scraggly wanted to take long walks and follow the ringing church bells. Grandpa Screecher, on the other hand, wanted to keep her locked up. He locked the gate from the outside, and once even tried to put her mother's chain on her. Scraggly bucked and refused, and Grandpa Screecher didn't insist. After all, the dogs had been stolen while the mother dog was chained up. 'Be careful, okay? Stay home.' Grandpa Screecher stepped through the gate and locked it behind him.

Scraggly went up to the gate and watched him leave. She felt lonely.

'So you want to get out, huh?' wheezed the old cat from the top of the wall. Lately, the cat wasn't acting quite like her old self. Yesterday she even slipped off the wall. 'The old start worrying about all kinds of things, but the young can't be stopped.'

'Shut up!' Scraggly parroted her mother. Now that she was the only one left, it was her responsibility to guard the house until her mother and siblings came home. She didn't want to listen to the cat's riddles. Even though the old feline put on airs about the depth of her knowledge, none of what she said actually made sense to Scraggly.

Scraggly looked up at the old shoe that Grandpa Screecher had tied to the top of the cage. She would never forget what had happened. When everyone returned home, she would tell them why that shoe was hanging there. She dozed off, but lifted her head when she heard music coming from the church. It trickled into the quiet yard, tickling her ears, whispering and urging her to come. She looked around. Where was the old cat? The acupuncturist's dog was whining faintly. He was always tied up because he had a predilection for wandering around and making trouble. Thankfully this meant he didn't peek in that often to bother her. He had wanted to chat to her but she could tell he was bad news. She flattened herself and crawled out through the bottom of the gate. Grandpa Screecher thought it was sufficient to lock the gate but he didn't realise she could still leave the yard like this. She never returned late from her walks; she sensed that Grandpa was nervous about leaving the house unoccupied after her family had been taken.

The music was calling her. She went towards the church, marking the ground. At first, she was just copying what Goldie used to do, but now it was a habit, her way of telling other dogs to keep their distance. Especially that silly dog at the acupuncturist's. She decided to avoid walking past that house today; that route took her towards the avenue and the embankment, and going there made her remember what had happened with her family, causing her hair to bristle and her chest to tighten.

Scraggly walked along the creek, listening to the music. Humming, she walked along the fields and the rice paddies, past the village meeting hall and the house with the pigs. Beyond the neighbourhood shop was a narrow intersection. Scraggly paused. She had never gone further than that on her own. She had gone to Grandpa Screecher's bicycle shop a few times with Grandma, but those were the only times she had ventured beyond where she was now.

She selected the path to the right, lined with houses. She came out on a hill dense with pine trees. Behind that was the church. She approached slowly. The music was coming from there, but who was making it? Scraggly felt on edge. All kinds of strange smells and sounds were swirling around her. The music stopped. Scraggly looked around. It was always like this; the music always stopped. Why did it stop?

'Hey, who's the hairy one?'

Scraggly turned around. A skinny spotted dog with long legs grinned as he approached and sniffed at her. 'What's your name? Where do you live? You look nice.'

It would be better to leave now. She hadn't come to make friends, especially not with a dog who seemed as unpleasant as this one. She turned to head back.

'Hey, you!' growled another dog, blocking her way. He

had a squashed head and stubby legs. Scraggly took a step back.

A brown stray, his fur rough and sleep in his eyes, ambled over. 'You're in our territory,' he said, flashing his teeth.

The dog with the squashed head took a step forward. 'And you're marking territory. You're just a female. You're asking for trouble.'

'We should teach her what we're about,' remarked the brown stray.

The dog with the squashed head came over, sniffing, and went behind Scraggly to investigate her. She sidled away in the direction of home.

The brown dog tensed his shoulders and came up to her, as did the spotted one. The spotted one was clearly not as confident as the other two. He stood behind one dog and then the other, not taking his eyes off her.

Scraggly felt her muscles tense. She would have to fight if they attacked her; she would never make it home if they thought she was a coward. 'I'm not bothering you,' she said gently, politely. She wanted to leave.

'You don't get it, do you?' the spotted dog scoffed. 'Your mere presence here is bothering us.'

The dog with the squashed head growled again. 'We have initiation rules here. You can't just come and go as you wish.' He lowered his body, flexing the muscles on his wide chest and legs.

The brown stray followed suit.

What would her mother do? What would Goldie do? She would fight if she had to, but she wanted to leave without any trouble. Her breathing grew rapid and her body stiffened.

The brown stray leaped in her direction. Scraggly closed her eyes. Her shoulder ached. Then she came to her senses: lowering her torso, she bent her body like a bow. 'Don't touch me!' she snarled.

She had been defeated so easily when the thief came to take her entire family. She wouldn't be taken like that again. She wasn't a puppy any more. She looked at each of the three dogs surrounding her. She had to win against one, preferably the leader. She bent her legs and decided to target the dog with the squashed head. He seemed the strongest and the most confident. She pretended to retreat, then reared and bit him on the neck. The others rushed at her.

'A dog fight! There's blood!' Little kids ran towards them.

'Get him! Get him!'

'That's so unfair, the hairy one is all alone!'

'It's the dog from the junk shop. We have to tell the junk shop man!'

Some kids picked up sticks to try to pry them apart, but most stood by, watching in terror. The four dogs rolled around as one. Scraggly's bones were being crushed. She had been bitten. She finally escaped the other dogs, her teeth sinking into the scruff of the dog with the squashed head, who was writhing.

Suddenly, the dogs retreated. Scraggly let go, momentarily confused. Some people had taken their shirts off and were flapping them at the tangle of dogs. But she thought she heard a dog ordering, 'Stop that at once!' She looked around, panting.

'I told you not to make trouble!' She hadn't imagined it. It was a deep, clear voice.

The brown stray and the spotted dog looked downcast. With lowered tails, they slunk off through the crowd. The dog with the squashed head backed away, nearly crawling. Scraggly peered through the hair covering her eyes. A white dog, the hair on his neck bristling, stood proudly in the crowd. He must be the leader of this area.

'That hairy dog is quite something! Whose is it?' exclaimed someone in the audience.

'That mutt really got a licking.'

Scraggly left slowly, her body aching. It hurt everywhere but she walked resolutely ahead without looking back. Her house was so far away. Tears sprang into her eyes.

'Are you all right?'

Scraggly turned around in surprise. It was the white dog. She dropped into attack mode again. Would she have to fight? But he was looking at her with an air of concern. The hair on his neck was lying flat. She relaxed.

'That was very dangerous,' he continued. 'You should avoid them.'

Scraggly shrugged. She had to get home. If only her mother and siblings were there, they might have licked her wounds and made her feel better.

'I've never met anyone like you before,' said the white dog. 'I've never seen a female fight like that.'

Scraggly was embarrassed, but the comment also piqued her anger. What was he talking about? Just because she was a female didn't mean she should stand by meekly and get beaten up. She felt like biting him, too.

The white dog came up to her. Without a word, he began to lick her wounds.

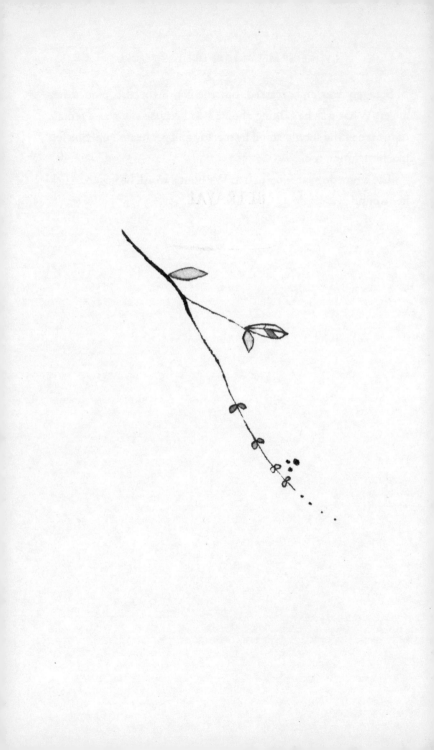

BETRAYAL

Scraggly licked the black pup.

'Don't, Scraggly. It's already dead.' Grandpa Screecher gently pushed away the cold, small puppy.

Scraggly sat down in dismay. He had been the smallest and weakest of the four in the litter. He had lived only two days.

'He looks like you,' Grandpa said sympathetically. 'I'm sorry that his life was only this long.'

Scraggly lowered her head. What had she done wrong? She had cleaned him. She'd made sure he didn't get hurt; when the others squirmed closer to her, she had ensured that they didn't crush him. But he'd trembled all the while, breathing weakly and moving slowly. More alarmingly, he hadn't smelled right. The others smelled sweet, but he had smelled sour from the very beginning.

Grandpa Screecher placed a bowl of seaweed soup in front of her. 'Eat up. You have to eat well to help your babies grow.'

If he was going to live for such a short time, why was he even

67

born? He hadn't even taken his first steps. Scraggly looked up at Grandpa Screecher sadly.

'This must be hard because it's your first birth,' Grandpa said. 'Puppies die from time to time. It's better this way. What if he grew up but was unable to do what he was supposed to?'

Scraggly whined, remembering her youngest sibling who had died in the vegetable garden. Would her dead baby be warmer if she licked him a little more?

Grandpa Screecher pointed at the soup. 'Scraggly, stop whining and eat!'

Scraggly licked his stiff hand. He stroked her neck gently. His caresses reminded her that though one was gone, she was blessed with three others, one white and two grey puppies. Scraggly got up slowly. The pups, who had been suckling, fell off, whimpering.

Grandpa Screecher exited the cage and closed the blanket-covered gate behind him. 'I was worried for no reason! Scraggly is a good breeder, I can tell.'

Scraggly ate her soup, thinking of the white dog. A long time had passed; spring was gone and the hot summer was waning. After that first encounter, she had never seen him again. She missed him. The puppies would grow up to be handsome, just like their father. The white pup especially looked just like his father, down to his pointy ears.

Scraggly stuck her nose in the pot and ate until she could see the bottom. She lay on her side and the pups felt their way to her belly. She gazed down at the squirming bundles. Three were too few. If the black one were here, she wouldn't feel an absence like this. She knew she would eventually feel at peace, though. How could such small, fragile beings breathe on their own? They each had their own warmth, too. For the first time since her mother and siblings had been taken away, she had a family of her own. Grandpa Screecher would bury her black pup under the persimmon tree; if he couldn't be her baby, he would become rich soil for the fruit. She drew in a deep breath. Even though the large cage was shrouded with blankets, she could smell everything outside. The old cat was there, probably dying to know what was going on in the cage. Scraggly twitched her nose and smiled, feeling superior. The old cat couldn't have babies, even though she acted as though she knew everything. Scraggly looked down at the puppies. She would keep them safe from the old cat. She wouldn't let anything happen to them. Her hair bristled just thinking about what had happened to Baby long ago. But she had nothing to worry about in the cage; Grandpa made sure she wouldn't be bothered. The blankets gave her privacy; he was the only one who brought her food. He kept the light bulb on all night so she could look after her babies.

Not long after, the babies opened their eyes. They were growing chubby. Soon, they were able to venture out of the cage.

'Children, don't go near the fence. Be careful with the cat next door. She looks old and harmless, but she's capable of anything,' warned Scraggly.

The old cat sneered each time. 'What do they know?'

*

Foul weather brought on a tragedy. One windy, overcast day, the puppies were safe inside the cage while the large apricot tree next to the kennel shook and thrashed, as did the camellia and persimmon trees in the garden. Leaves were torn off branches and flew about. The trees swayed and rocked, unable to stand straight. Black clouds converged overhead. Windows shook and the slate tiles on Grandpa Screecher's roof rattled precariously.

The pups huddled together, trembling and whimpering. 'I'm scared,' they all said.

Scraggly paced in and out of her kennel, waiting anxiously for Grandpa Screecher. With each gust, the slate roof heaved. The lush pumpkin leaves climbing the wall rustled and shivered. A large pumpkin fell off the vine.

Scraggly barked anxiously. A sudden gust of wind flipped a large number of slate tiles off the roof. The roof reared like an angry snake. The tiles blew straight off and slammed into the neighbour's house, smashing everywhere.

Scraggly retreated into her kennel and curled up. She had never seen anything like this. Rain began pouring down. A stream formed by the flower garden. Torn-off leaves coasted along the flowing water and flooded the vegetable patch. Fat raindrops pounded on the roof of Scraggly's kennel. She covered her head with her front paws. Eventually the wind died down. Grandpa Screecher came home. Scraggly was glad to see him but there was nothing he could do. He got soaked trying to secure the remaining part of the roof.

The storm was over by morning. Everything was a mess.

Grandpa Screecher looked around, frowning. Their neighbour came by to complain about the damage caused to her roof by Grandpa Screecher's tiles. 'It'll be fine once a few tiles are replaced,' she remarked. 'You can include ours when you get someone to come and fix yours.'

Grandpa Screecher sighed but answered confidently, 'Definitely.'

'Thanks, that would be great.'

To Scraggly, she sounded just like her old cat: a little cold and demanding.

'Damn,' Grandpa Screecher grumbled after the neighbour had left. 'That's going to be expensive. I haven't paid for everything in the junk shop yet, and I can't ask Chanu for help, since the sign on his shop was smashed in the bad weather.' He chain-smoked, his face furrowed. He gazed through the smoke at the puppies frolicking in the debris-strewn vegetable patch.

The next day, Grandpa Screecher put a chain around Scraggly's neck. She reared and barked, trying to convey to him that she would stay out of his way if he let her be. But he tied her to a pillar. She wasn't happy about it, but she understood; he must need her out of the way to clean up the yard.

Then a man stepped through the gates.

Scraggly's eyes bulged. She started barking ferociously. It was the thief. She lunged and growled.

The man flinched, but recovered his obsequious smile. 'I can tell they're from a good bloodline.'

'How much for all three?' Grandpa Screecher asked bluntly, grimacing.

Scraggly stared at Grandpa, uncomprehending.

The man smirked. 'You're not selling the big one?'

'No, I have to keep her. She's the breeder.'

'They're fine, but they're just puppies,' sniffed the man.

Scraggly's heart sank. Grandpa Screecher was selling all her pups?

'Look here, Kim,' Grandpa said gruffly. 'I know dogs. You can't find puppies like this anywhere. I wouldn't be doing this if it weren't for my roof.'

Not her babies! Scraggly lunged. The chain pulled her tight as she tried to bite the dog trader. Her nails clawed the ground. She couldn't get near him. She frothed at the mouth.

The dog trader didn't blink. Grandpa Screecher wasn't even looking her way. She would tear to shreds anyone who touched her babies.

The dog trader shot Scraggly a look. 'A real piece of work, that mongrel.'

How dare he! Scraggly's eyes burned. Her chest felt tight. How could Grandpa Screecher betray her like this?

'Watch your words,' warned Grandpa Screecher. 'Dogs understand everything you say.'

The dog trader laughed. 'Is that right?'

'You don't think she knows that her puppies are going to be taken away? I'll sell them to you for a good price, so let's keep it brief. I'm not happy about this either.' Grandpa Screecher went towards the cage.

The puppies burst into tears. Scraggly leaped and tugged. She should have bitten the dog trader harder when she'd had the chance. She should have kept her grip on him until the very end.

'What's the point of taking dogs that aren't big enough?' mumbled the dog trader, but he followed Grandpa Screecher. He stopped when he spotted the old shoe hanging on the cage. He glanced at Scraggly. 'Actually, yes, I'll take them. I – I know they're from good stock.'

GRANDPA SCREECHER'S FOREARM

Scraggly was tied up and shut in the cage. Her bowl was full of food but she hadn't touched it. She paced, her chain rattling. She didn't take her eyes off Grandpa Screecher, who was busy fixing the roof. He had hired men to fix the neighbour's roof but was repairing his own. Scraggly growled, unable to forgive him. She wanted her babies back. She was hoarse from shouting and barking, but she refused to stop.

The old cat walked up and down the top of the wall. 'Listen to yourself. Now you really sound frightful. This is what life is, you know. You say goodbye, they die, and life goes on. I know how it goes. I've never known a dog who lived with all her pups.'

'Shut up!' Scraggly shouted.

'I'm telling you, it's no use. You know what that old man is like. Dogs are pocket money for him. They're gone, Scraggly. They're never coming back. Ever.'

'Shut up, I said!'

'Goodness, my ears! All right, do what you want. I'm just trying to help. I'm trying to be a good neighbour. You're really so very dense sometimes.' The cat leaped off the wall.

Was this winter's doing again? She didn't want to listen to that stupid old cat, but she had to wonder why winter brought her such bad things. Scraggly continued to pace, breathing raggedly. If she weren't tied up and in this cage, she would bound over to Grandpa Screecher and bite him. He was crouching, his back to her. She hated him.

Grandpa Screecher had been welding all morning to secure the slate roof. He smelled more metallic than usual. Sparks flew; bluish smoke hung in the air. Scraggly heard the music coming from the church. It sounded very far away. Her heart ached. Sorrow rushed up from inside her. She remembered how she'd felt when she met the white dog. She remembered how her mother had looked up at the sky and howled when Baby died. She felt she knew how her mother must have felt. She looked up at the sky, like her mother, and howled.

'Shut up, Scraggly!' Grandpa Screecher shouted.

Ignoring him, Scraggly howled even louder and longer.

'Shut up! A dog making those sounds brings bad luck.'

Scraggly continued.

'You little—' Grandpa Screecher put down his welding tools and stood up.

Scraggly kept howling obstinately. Stupid old man. He had given all her babies to the thief. How could he have done such a thing?

'You barked all night long so nobody could sleep. Now you're really pushing my patience to the limit.' Grandpa Screecher pushed the black face shield up onto his head and glared at her.

Scraggly wasn't afraid. She glared right back and howled again; this was the only way she could get him to look at her.

'Damn it,' snapped Grandpa Screecher. 'I told you to shut up! You're getting on my nerves.'

Scraggly refused to stop. She was angry. This was unfair.

Grandpa Screecher's face was red as he strode over. He picked up the broom leaning on the persimmon tree. 'How dare you!' He opened the cage and brought the broom down onto Scraggly. She had never seen him look so ferocious.

Scraggly avoided the blows, barking, glaring and baring her teeth. Her heart throbbed with each blow to her back, behind and calves. The chain was tight around her neck. It would have been better if the thief had taken her along with her mother and siblings.

'You're bringing this house bad luck!' shouted Grandpa Screecher. She couldn't forgive him.

'Dogs that act like this get killed,' warned Grandpa Screecher.

Then do it, Scraggly thought belligerently. She jumped up and bit him on the arm. He screamed and fell to his knees. He threw an arm around her neck. She didn't let go. He was moaning. If Dongi and his father hadn't stepped into the yard right at that moment, she would have broken his arm.

'Father!' Chanu ran up and shoved a stick into Scraggly's mouth to force open her jaws. She glanced at Dongi, who was staring at her in a daze. Scraggly caught his round black eyes and tears welled in her eyes.

'You beast! How could you bite your master?' Chanu grabbed Scraggly by the neck.

Grandpa pointed at Scraggly. 'Cut off some fur,' he moaned.

'What? What for?'

'Do it.'

'Oh, Father, not that superstitious stuff,' Chanu protested. 'We have to go to the hospital.'

'It's fine. Do it.'

'What if it gets infected?' Chanu argued.

'She's up to date with her injections. It'll be fine.'

'Dongi, go and get some scissors or a knife!' Chanu shouted, his hand a vice around her snout.

Dongi stood frozen to the spot, staring at Scraggly. Grandpa Screecher leaned on the fence, cradling his forearm, sweating, watching her.

'Go!' Chanu yelled.

Dongi startled and ran to the toolbox. He rummaged around but ran back empty-handed.

'There's a pair of scissors,' Chanu said gently. 'Go and find them.'

Dongi went back, on the verge of tears, and brought the scissors.

Chanu cut off a handful of fur from Scraggly's neck. It didn't hurt but Scraggly trembled, not understanding what was happening. Grandpa Screecher held his hand out. He left the cage. Chanu inched away from Scraggly, then dashed out and locked the gate. 'It looks serious. We should go to the hospital.'

'After I do this,' Grandpa Screecher insisted. He burned the handful of fur. He placed the singed hair on his wound and tied it with a piece of cloth. The scorched smell wafted along on the wind. Scraggly hadn't realised that a terrible smell was hiding in her own fur.

'You're so mean!' yelled Dongi, standing on the other side of the cage. 'Why did you bite my grandpa?'

Scraggly felt dazed. She didn't know what to think. She paced, dragging her chain on the cement floor of the cage.

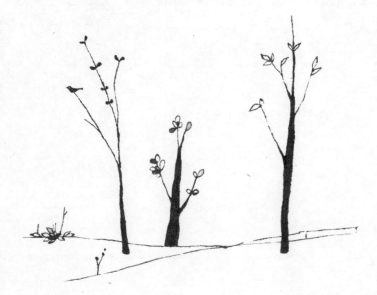

UNCERTAIN DAYS

Grandpa Screecher looked at Scraggly lying outside his shop as he put together a bicycle wheel. 'I said, go home,' he ordered, pushing his reading glasses up the bridge of his nose.

Scraggly glanced at him. She closed her eyes. During the winter she wandered around town before going home, but now that she was heavier she followed Grandpa Screecher out in the morning and spent all day at the shop. She didn't want to be home alone.

Grandpa Screecher no longer tried to tie Scraggly up. Only when he stopped chaining her did she calm down and start putting on some weight. While she was shut up in the cage and tied to the pole, though she'd looked big at first glance, her fur woolly and thick, she had teetered on the brink of anaemia and been in a foul mood. She'd refused to even look at the bowl of food that Grandpa placed under her nose. Finally, he shook his head. 'I give up,' he said, and untied her.

When her legs grew stronger, Scraggly followed the music to the church. The next time she went further. She couldn't stay still. Her heart was drained of emotion and she felt alone. Each time she left home, she hoped she would bump into the white dog, but she never did. Instead, she met a brown dog that had some hunting-dog blood. That was how she became large with puppies again.

Grandpa Screecher frowned. 'You'll be giving birth soon. You have to stay close to home, otherwise you'll end up having babies in the street.' He slid the spokes into the wheel horizontally and tightened the screws, then laid the rim down and pushed the oilcloth off his lap. He opened the half-closed glass sliding door, which made a terrible high-pitched sound, and stepped outside.

Scraggly got to her feet laboriously only when he was standing directly in front of her. Her belly was large; she was slow to move.

'You stubborn thing,' Grandpa Screecher muttered, gently pushing her along.

She slapped his hand with her tail and walked slowly away. There was nowhere to go and nothing she could do. She wished she could have her babies somewhere better. She turned the corner at the National Agricultural Cooperative. The old cat leaped lightly down from the tall ventilation window. 'No luck today either?'

Scraggly kept walking. The old cat grinned and followed her, giving off a pungent smell. Scraggly ignored her.

'Get your head out of the clouds,' the cat advised. 'Why are you always wandering? There's no place better than home.'

'Mind your own business.'

'You think I'm a joke, I see. Every time I say something import-ant, you brush me off. I've lived a long time, you know. I know things.'

Scraggly glared at the cat, who stepped back a few paces.

'I've had many babies too,' continued the cat. 'So many. I can't even remember how many. I was just like you about my babies.'

'And?' snapped Scraggly.

'Now none of them is here. They've all left. I lived with some of them until they were older, but they're all gone. That's what happens.'

'Not to me.'

'What makes you think you're any different?' asked the cat. 'Some kittens were sold, with a ribbon around their neck like they were presents. Some died. One left without even telling me. Ingrate! I loved him so much, but he never came back. Uh-oh ...' The old cat flinched and crouched.

A fight was brewing in the empty lot at the end of the path. Four dogs circled a lone dog in the middle. Scraggly gasped. The white dog was at the centre. Her heart leaped. She thought of all the puppies she'd lost. Here was their father, standing just down the road, the very dog who had never left her thoughts. He was cornered. How could he be cornered? She could tell something very bad was about to happen. She went closer, her body tensed. The four dogs around him looked ready to pounce. A brown one looked particularly vicious.

'Scraggly,' whispered the old cat, 'let's get out of here!'

Scraggly never appreciated the cat's opinions, expressed in such a syrupy voice. She especially didn't want to hear them now. She had to help the white dog, the way he had helped her.

'Don't get involved,' said the cat sharply. 'Think about your condition!'

Scraggly ignored her.

The four dogs moved faster. The white dog looked ready, though he was facing strong opposition. Then they sprang at him.

Scraggly hesitated. The five dogs were tangled in a heap, dust flying everywhere. They leaped and rolled. Growls and shrieks pierced the air. The white dog was swift but there were too many dogs going at him. Scraggly moved in slowly, in attack mode. She watched for a chance to dive in. She couldn't tell who had bitten whom but the white dog appeared to be at the bottom of the pile. She stomped her feet and barked. Nobody took any notice. She paced. The moment had come: she ran into the tussle. She bit whomever she could reach, then someone bit her on the thigh and hung on.

'Let go!' Scraggly twisted her body. Her belly tightened. She couldn't breathe. She couldn't see. She was frozen, unable to budge. Something was wrong. She fell into a dip in the road, her tumble cushioned by overgrown grass. Someone fell on top of her.

She gathered her wits about her, but she couldn't get up.

'Enough!' The brown dog stepped back.

The white dog didn't let go of the dog he had between his jaws. That dog was squirming, splayed on the ground. Everyone was scratched and bloodied and bedraggled.

'Fine. I know you're strong,' said the brown dog.

The white dog finally let go.

The brown dog nodded at Scraggly and smirked. 'If it weren't for her we could have kept going.'

The white dog looked at Scraggly, angry and ferocious. She looked away.

The four dogs left together, swaggering as they went.

The white dog's shoulders drooped. 'You should have stayed away,' he admonished. 'I know you were trying to help but you humiliated me. The leader stands alone and retreats alone.'

Scraggly's chest felt tight. Had she got him demoted? The white dog ambled away. He hadn't even asked if she was all right. She tried to stand but her forelegs buckled. The wound on her thigh throbbed. She tried to lick it but she couldn't reach around her belly. And her belly felt so tight. Were the babies inside frightened?

Grandpa Screecher had complained that she would end up having her babies in the street. Even the cat had warned her to take care of herself. She suddenly grew afraid. The day was waning. How would she get home? Soon, it became very dark. Cars and bicycles passed occasionally but nobody spotted Scraggly lying to the side of the road. She howled so Grandpa Screecher could hear her. She did that several times but nobody came. The night deepened. Her body ached and trembled. Was this how she was going to die? She wanted to go home. She hadn't felt this bruised and battered in a long time. She howled again. Would anyone hear her? She was feeling weaker. Was this the end? She shivered. Her eyes kept closing. The dust and the cold night air had dried her nose and her throat was parched.

'Scraggly?'

A familiar voice. Her heart leaped into her throat.

Grandpa Screecher felt his way towards her. He tried to pick her up but she was too heavy. 'Why would you do this, huh?' His voice was exasperated but his touch was gentle. His warm hand stroked her belly. She finally felt at ease.

'Wait here. I'll be back soon.'

Scraggly laid her head down. Sleep overcame her. She woke as Grandpa Screecher was struggling to pick her up. He placed her in his cart. 'I've never met such a stubborn dog,' he moaned. 'It's like when Chanu was younger and drove me crazy! You're untamable. How can I not be worried? You don't listen!'

Listening to Grandpa Screecher grouse, Scraggly bumped along in the cart and fell into a deep slumber.

KORI THE RASCAL

'Put Kori away, won't you?' Grandma swung her spoon to shoo the puppy away. 'Look, her fur is getting into my soybeans.'

Mischievous Kori scampered away but returned to steal more boiled beans.

'Don't you put your snout in there!' Grandma raised her spoon again.

Kori scurried off.

Scraggly was hungry for beans too, but she didn't dare mimic her pup. It wasn't that she was afraid of Grandma, it was that she felt awkward around Grandpa Screecher. Scraggly wasn't young enough to act like a puppy and things were strained between them. She knew she wouldn't be able to hold back if Grandpa Screecher thrashed her again, so she was always careful not to make even the smallest mistake.

'Put her away or tie her up, like I keep telling you,' insisted Grandma.

'Put her in the cage? You want to sit here listening to all the whimpering? Just hurry up and finish what you're doing.' Grandpa laughed as he tied the napa cabbage in the vegetable garden.

Kori got into everything – she ate ravenously, ran around, and made a mess of things. But she was a beautiful dog; she looked just like her father. Grandpa Screecher was partial to her. He had sold seven puppies but kept Kori, the strongest, best-looking pup. Scraggly was pleased; she was getting to watch her grow up.

'Be good, Kori,' admonished Scraggly from her spot in front of her kennel.

Kori ran into the vegetable patch, barking loudly. She skidded to a stop in front of the pumpkin vine. The old cat shrieked and jumped up onto the wall; she had fallen off while dozing. 'Teach that kid some manners!' she grumbled.

Scraggly laughed. So did Grandpa Screecher and Grandma.

'Scraggly, don't raise a puppy to behave like that,' the cat complained.

Scraggly shrugged. 'What can I do? Can't you look after yourself?'

'That rascal won't even let me nap.' The old cat left in a huff.

'We should be getting a good crop of persimmons,' mused Grandpa. 'That tree is already seven years old.'

'We should give Yeongseon a bigger bunch,' Grandma reminded Grandpa as she pounded the cooked beans in a mortar and shaped them into bricks. 'Last year she was upset that she didn't get many. She's the one who planted the tree in the first place.'

Grandpa Screecher trimmed the cabbage he had harvested from

the vegetable garden. Kori sniffed it. A worm squirmed out near the roots, and she leaped back in surprise.

'The owner of the tree shouldn't feel left out,' continued Grandma. 'She's the one who planted it when she had her first baby. The tree will grow better if the owner feels good about it.'

'Nobody owns a tree,' scoffed Grandpa Screecher. 'Sharing the fruit is enough. And I always give her the prettiest ones! I pick the reddest ones without scratches, since she's my only girl.'

'Oh, do you?' smirked Grandma.

'Hurry up and make me some kimchi. You're the one who made this appointment even when I said I didn't need one. I have to be there on time.'

'Are you stopping off at Chanu's shop first?'

'Of course,' Grandpa Screecher replied. 'I have to go all the way into town! I'm sure they're all out of kimchi. And last time Dongi left his robot here. He can't live without it.'

'That's not the important thing,' Grandma mumbled, her face darkening.

For a while, the couple worked without speaking. Grandpa Screecher smoked as he trimmed shallots and Grandma salted the cabbage and laid out the smooth bricks of beans on a tall, straw-covered shady platform to dry. Kori wouldn't be able to get to them up there.

Grandma finished in the afternoon, although she worked fast without taking a break. Grandpa was impatient, having already changed into his nice clothes. 'How slow can you be? I'm not the one who made the appointment at the hospital. You're taking forever!'

'Goodness! I'm done now. Stop nagging.'

'I'm not nagging. Look, the sun's practically setting.' Grandpa Screecher placed the jar of fresh kimchi on the back of his bicycle, muttering under his breath. He wheeled it out and rode off, his jacket flapping in the wind. He looked carefree, like a child.

Grandma finally relaxed and sat down in Grandpa Screecher's comfortable chair in the yard just below the veranda. 'I hope everything's okay ...'

Kori put her front paws in her lap, begging to be picked up. Scraggly watched Grandma's preoccupied expression; the persimmon leaves swayed in the breeze and shaded her face occasionally. Something bad was looming. Scraggly barked loudly to ward it off, whatever it was.

Grandma looked at Scraggly, then at the basins and bowls strewn about the yard. 'Goodness, I'm not even done yet! I have to feed all of you, too. And now the phone is ringing. Wait, I'll be back.' She got up, rubbed her aching lower back and disappeared inside.

Kori took one of her shoes and settled down to chew on it, even though she was bound to get into trouble when Grandma returned.

Scraggly ambled over and nudged her. 'Don't ruin it.'

Kori frowned and shook her head. 'It's not as tasty as the beans. I want more of those.'

'She'll feed us soon.' Scraggly sprawled under the chair. Kori came over and snuggled next to her, her head nestled against Scraggly's stomach.

They could hear Grandma on the phone inside. 'He's been

having diarrhoea, but there's nothing seriously wrong with him. His appetite isn't what it used to be ... yes, of course it would be nice to have you visit. It's been a long time since I've seen you, Sister-in-Law! Yes, yes ...'

Kori's eyes twinkled with curiosity. 'Mum, what's a sister-in-law?'

'A sister-in-law? Well ...' Scraggly lifted her head and blinked. She had never heard that word before. 'Oh, it's a good thing. A very good thing.'

The old cat guffawed from the top of the wall and rested her head on her front paws. 'Did you say it was a good thing? Scraggly, if you don't know, just say so.'

'It's rude to listen in on conversations!' snapped Kori.

Scraggly smiled – her daughter took after her. With her short, shiny fur, Kori was more handsome, but she was forthright and curious, just like Scraggly.

'You're the rude one,' the old cat said. 'Is it a crime to have excellent hearing? Kids these days ... Just you wait, you little rascal. I'm going to get you.'

'I'd like to see you try,' Kori scoffed. 'Go ahead. I'll bite you!'

The old cat tutted. 'I should have known. I can't talk sense into animals who go about their days looking down at the ground.' She yawned.

Scraggly looked warily at those sharp teeth. Even though the cat was old and sometimes fell off the wall while dozing, you never could tell when she might bite.

'Who wants to come to the poultry farm with me?' called Grandma.

Kori scampered along, wagging her tail. Scraggly accompanied them as far as the gate and then watched Grandma walk out with her pup, holding a basket in one hand. Scraggly watched the two of them as they went along the embankment surrounding the field. Blood rushed to her head. She felt dizzy. Was it the sun? Kori ran ahead then fell behind; to Scraggly, she looked as though she were twinkling, as though she were floating on air.

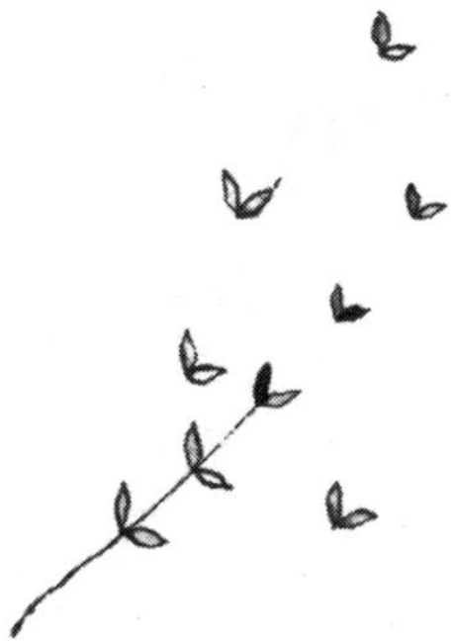

SISTER-IN-LAW

'Oh, my dear brother,' the guest said, holding Grandpa Screecher's hands, 'how are you feeling?'

'I'm fine!' Grandpa Screecher crowed, grinning. 'You didn't get motion sickness on the train?'

'The trains are so pleasant these days. The ride was comfortable.'

Scraggly had never seen Grandpa Screecher look so excited. She and Kori stared at the large box the guest had set down. It was tied with rope and there was a hole in the top; a hen with reddish-brown feathers and a clearly defined comb was poking her head out of the hole. The hen's eyes, however, were cloudy, and her neck was bent. She seemed near death.

Kori crept up and nudged the box. 'So this is Sister-in-Law!' exclaimed the pup.

'I brought sweet rice and a chicken. They'll revive you,' the guest was explaining. 'Boil them together for a long time. The broth will do you some good. I would have brought more but it was so heavy! I had all this on my head, and I felt like my neck was going to snap.' She untied the rope, opened the box, and lifted the chicken out.

The hen flopped over, curled her claws and shuddered.

'You brought all this rice!' cried Grandpa Screecher. 'But I know how hard you worked to grow it. This must be a *mal* and a half at least! And this hen – isn't this your brood hen?'

'And what if it is? If it's good for your health ...'

'It's not too perky, is it? Is it going to pop its clogs?' Grandpa Screecher nudged the hen, who opened her eyes and closed them again.

'Oh, it's just a country hen,' the guest said airily. 'First time on a train, so it's probably just motion sickness.'

Grandpa Screecher laughed.

Scraggly and Kori stuck close to the hen. Scraggly soon grew bored but Kori kept poking the hen. The hen just blinked.

As the sun began to set, Kori suddenly shouted, 'Sister-in-Law has come back to life!'

It was true. The hen had recovered and was wandering the yard. The guest had left already, but the hen didn't look for her. She seemed to be right at home.

'I can't do it, you handle it.' Grandma handed Grandpa Screecher a knife.

Shocked, Scraggly and Kori stepped back.

Frowning, Grandpa Screecher took the knife and stared at the hen.

'Do it now so I can cook it tonight,' urged Grandma. 'Then you can eat it tomorrow.'

Grandpa Screecher nodded. But he sat on the platform and just kept watching. He stayed like that until it was completely dark. Only then did Grandpa Screecher run after the hen. The hen slipped away each time, leaping from one big earthenware pot to the next, coasting along, flapping her wings.

'Wow, Sister-in-Law!' Kori ran around, excited. 'You're amazing!'

It was too much for Scraggly. She went into her kennel and watched from there. The old cat laughed and laughed on top of the wall.

Finally, Grandpa Screecher managed to catch the hen by the wing. 'My god, am I out of breath! I've got you now.' He trapped the hen under an overturned bucket. He went to the shed, panting, and took out a length of rope. The hen was fluttering so energetically that the bucket kept heaving. Grandpa slid the chicken out and tied the rope around her neck. 'I can't kill this hen,' grumbled Grandpa Screecher as he tied the other end of the rope to a persimmon tree branch.

The hen fluttered and flapped, waving her claws as though to scratch the air.

Kori barked in sympathy under the tree. Scraggly joined her uneasily.

'I'll have to leave you here for now.' Grandpa brushed his hands off and went inside.

'Mum, why is he doing that to Sister-in-Law?' asked Kori.

The old cat cut in, laughing. 'She won't be here in the morning.' She groomed her whiskers and licked her claws. Her voice sounded more sinister than usual, and she smelled more pungent tonight.

'You're not planning anything, are you?' asked Scraggly warily.

'Who, me? Not me. But the night ... the night might do something.'

'Don't you dare,' warned Scraggly. 'I'll be watching. Don't even dream of it.'

'Oh, I'm so scared,' mocked the old cat. 'Why would I dare, anyway? You glow when the moon rises. You'll be watching me? Oh, what *will* I do?'

'I glow? When the moon rises?' Scraggly wasn't sure if the old cat was making fun of her.

'That's why I like you, you know,' confided the old cat. 'You're different.'

'What do you mean, you like me?'

'Well, what I mean is – you're not bad, considering you're a dog,' allowed the old cat.

'I glow?'

'At night, you look bluish. It's probably because I have such good eyesight. They're still sharp, you see! I come from excellent stock, even by feline standards ... '

'Bluish? Stop it. Don't make fun of me,' retorted Scraggly.

'All right, don't believe me. One knows the least about oneself.'

Scraggly bristled. 'You know nothing but you act like you know everything. Why would someone from such an excellent line of cats be wandering around peeking into other people's houses?'

'I'm just taking a walk,' the old cat said sullenly.

'Cat voices always sound so smooth,' Scraggly murmured to herself. 'But don't forget about the hidden teeth.' She stared at the wall. She dozed off from time to time but spent most of the night awake until it was nearing dawn. Her eyes stayed fixed on the wall, but nothing happened while she kept watch.

Suddenly, there was a commotion. What was going on? Scraggly barked under the persimmon tree. She could tell that the hen and the old cat were tussling. But she couldn't see more than shadows as it was not yet daytime. Wings flapped and someone was breathing hard. The sounds were all confused to Scraggly's ears. She caught a whiff of blood. It was all happening mid-air. Then everything stopped. Someone was injured, but she couldn't tell who.

'Cock-a-doodle-doo!'

Just half an hour later the sun was rising; it was morning. The sound was coming from the persimmon tree. The hen was flapping and crowing like a rooster. 'Cock-a-doodle-doo!' The rope was still looped around the hen's neck, but with her chest puffed out in pride, the rope looked like a medal.

'What's wrong with your face?' asked Kori, addressing the top of the wall.

Scraggly turned to look. The old cat was perched on the wall, covered in scratches and blood. The cat glared sullenly at the hen crowing and fluttering about.

'Hey, kid,' called the hen. 'You called me Sister-in-Law, right? I'll take it.' She pushed her chest out again and nodded, pleased.

THOSE WHO ARE LEFT AND
THOSE WHO LEAVE

Scraggly was chained up again, though she bucked and leaped. It was because she had bitten Sister-in-Law so hard that she almost killed the hen. With Scraggly subdued, Sister-in-Law became smug and arrogant, especially when they overheard Grandpa Screecher telling Grandma that he was thinking of bringing home a rooster.

'No, Sister-in-Law!' yelled Kori. 'That's mine!'

Ignoring the puppy, Sister-in-Law took over Kori's bowl and fended her off. She pecked at the food. Since Sister-in-Law had joined the family, Kori was always going hungry. Kori inched closer to her bowl. Sister-in-Law raised her head in warning. Kori snuck her snout into the dish.

'Hey!' Sister-in-Law pecked Kori on the nose.

Kori screamed and fell back, her snout bloodied. This was the second time. The first time it happened, Scraggly had rushed at Sister-in-Law, almost biting her wing off. Kori went crying to her mother, hiding behind her.

'Leave that bowl alone, you thug!' Scraggly demanded.

'Did you just call me a thug?'

'You heard me. Look what you did to her!'

'I just wanted to eat from a bowl, too,' the hen shot back. 'I'm a guest in this household. How could you let a guest eat what is strewn on the ground?'

'A guest? You were almost dinner,' scoffed Scraggly.

The hen ignored her and continued. 'Actually, I'm not a guest any more, I'm a valuable member of the family. I'll be laying eggs for Grandpa and Grandma, so you have to treat me well.'

'You should have become soup a long time ago,' muttered Scraggly.

'Oh, please. You think I'm that easy?' Sister-in-Law didn't back down.

Scraggly tugged and strained at her chain, incensed. Sister-in-Law continued to peck at Kori's food without blinking. Since she had been yammering with her mouth full, the rice had splattered all around the bowl. If only she hadn't been tied down, Scraggly would have finished her off with a single bite. Then again, it was impossible to catch Sister-in-Law. She could leap and even glide from place to place when needed, and could easily breach the top of the wall. Even the old cat ceded her usual place and stalked the rooftops instead, though Sister-in-Law could flutter up to the roof too. The hen loved to look down at the neighbourhood, then land spectacularly in the yard. She dug in the yard when she was hungry, and she pecked Kori when she was bored. Kori spent most of her time avoiding Sister-in-Law.

'Any time I get a chance,' mumbled the old cat from the roof. 'Just you wait ... ' But she didn't approach, wary as she was of an attack.

The phone began to ring from inside the house, as it had done intermittently since early that morning. It stopped before starting up once more, then fell silent before it grew loud again. But Grandpa Screecher was at the shop and Grandma was out selling fish. The phone stopped ringing.

'He'll bring home a rooster for me,' remarked Sister-in-Law, spreading out her wings. 'When the rooster is here, you'll all be terrified!' Sister-in-Law flew up onto the persimmon tree. 'Grandpa's coming!'

He was coming back already? In the middle of the day? Scraggly hadn't noticed his metallic scent, as she had been concentrating solely on Sister-in-Law.

Grandpa Screecher walked in without his bicycle. He was pale and unsteady on his feet.

'What about the rooster? Where is he?' Sister-in-Law ran around Grandpa Screecher.

Something was wrong. He looked like he was about to topple over. Grandpa Screecher approached his chair slowly and sat down gingerly. He leaned back and closed his eyes.

'How could he come back empty-handed? How could he?' Sister-in-Law paced in front of Grandpa Screecher in a huff. When he didn't pay her any attention, she flounced off to the flowerbed and dug around, causing dust to fly up around her.

The phone began to ring again. But Grandpa Screecher

didn't move. Was he just resting? Had he fallen asleep? Grandpa Screecher's head leaned to the side and his arm hung below the chair. The persimmon leaves cast a shadow over his face.

Chanu stepped into the yard. Scraggly pricked up her ears, but she settled down when she didn't see Dongi. Chanu glanced at his father before rushing inside to answer the phone. He came out after a long time, looking concerned. 'This is going to be a shock to him, going to a specialist,' mumbled Chanu, looking up at the sky. He leaned down, studying his father in slumber. In a gentle voice, he woke him up. He helped Grandpa Screecher to his feet and led him indoors.

The next morning, Chanu and Grandpa Screecher emerged from the house together. Grandpa Screecher's eyes were sunken and dark. He looked even paler than he had the day before.

'It's too much,' Chanu protested. 'You have to buy them food. You won't be able to look after them. Why don't you get rid of them?'

Scraggly cocked her head. Something wasn't right.

'You need to focus on your own health,' continued Chanu.

Grandpa Screecher settled in his chair and lit a cigarette.

'Father, the doctor said no more smoking.'

'It's a lifelong habit. What am I supposed to do? I feel fine. The medicine's working. All this fuss over an upset stomach ...' Grandpa Screecher inhaled but burst out coughing. He had to stub out the cigarette. He let out a long sigh. 'I can't sell both of them. The house will be empty. A house has to have kids crying and food cooking, and we have nothing other than two old folks.'

'Father, really.'

'It'll feel too quiet if we don't even have a dog.' Grandpa Screecher gazed at Scraggly.

Scraggly stared back at him. Grandpa Screecher had already sold so many of her puppies. Only Kori remained. But now it sounded as if either Kori or she would be sold, never to return. Her heart was in her throat.

'Which one do you want to keep, the mother or the pup?' Chanu asked.

Grandpa Screecher didn't answer and Chanu didn't press him. Scraggly's throat was dry.

Even though he looked sickly, Grandpa Screecher did his work. He swept the yard, weeded the flowerbed and watered the vegetable garden. He fed the dogs. 'Eat up, Scraggly,' he said, pouring beef soup in her bowl. He stroked her head. Kori was given kibble.

Scraggly's throat closed up. She was the one being sold. Tears sprang to her eyes. She looked sadly at Grandpa Screecher, who looked away. Where would she go? What would happen to her? At least young Kori would stay.

Sister-in-Law approached Scraggly's bowl, suddenly uninterested in Kori's food.

'Get lost!' snapped Grandpa Screecher. He picked the hen up and heaved her away. She landed on the ground, fluttering and squawking as though she were dying.

The old cat snickered from the top of the wall. Scraggly went into her kennel and curled up. Kori followed her in and curled up against her. It was tight in there but Scraggly felt comforted.

'Mum, I think something bad is going to happen,' Kori said falteringly.

Scraggly licked her puppy's face with her dry, rough tongue. 'Yes, I think you're right.'

'What's going to happen?'

Scraggly sighed. So many things had gone wrong in her life. For some reason she had believed that nothing else would happen to her. But winter must have something more in store for her. What was it going to do to her now? She took a deep breath, but carefully, so that Kori wouldn't get nervous.

'The big one?' said a voice outside. 'Oh, that *sapsal* mix?' It was the dog trader.

Scraggly's nerves stood to attention. Fear bubbled up inside her. She was being sold to him? She shot out of the kennel, barking. Sister-in-Law, who had been eating her fill from Scraggly's bowl, fluttered away.

The dog trader had his bicycle with the wire cage on the back. He glanced at Scraggly.

'Don't send me off with him!' Scraggly yelled. Her heart was being clawed to shreds. Each time she barked, her throat felt as though it was raw.

'How am I going to catch her? Mind you, she's really something,' the dog trader said, laughing. 'If she were a pure breed, she'd be quite a specimen.'

Grandpa Screecher and Chanu didn't answer. Grandpa watched Scraggly as she leaped around.

'I'll have to come back next year for the puppy,' the dog trader said with a shrug. 'It'll be a while until that one's ready to be a breeder.'

Scraggly's stomach sank. She had forgotten about Kori. She couldn't let Kori go. That would be even worse. Why did this have to happen to her?

'It's strange,' commented Grandpa Screecher. 'She can't stand you.'

'Oh, you know. Dogs are like that.'

'I suppose so. You're like the grim reaper.'

The dog trader's smile faded. His cheek twitched with annoyance.

Grandpa Screecher turned and sat in his chair. He stared at Scraggly again. She kept barking.

The dog trader stood there, displeased. 'Look, if you're not going to sell, I have other places I need to be.'

'Take that one,' Grandpa Screecher said, nodding at Kori.

The world spun. Scraggly howled. Grandpa Screecher had to know that staying behind and leaving were equally unbearable, but he didn't look at her. He lit a cigarette but coughed so hard that he doubled over. Scraggly pulled on her chain, leaping and lunging, but the dog trader grabbed her puppy and shut her in the wire cage. Kori wailed. Scraggly barked and barked. This was just like the time her mother and siblings had been shoved in the cage and taken away. Kori's black eyes found her mother's. Her face was pressed against the wire of the cage. She looked dazed with terror.

'I gave you a good price, since you're a regular,' the dog trader said brusquely before leaving.

Scraggly chewed on her chain; it clanged against her teeth, ringing in her head. Kori's tearful whimpers came over the wall. Scraggly called back.

Unfathomably, the world turned quiet again.

THE COMING OF SORROW

Grandpa Screecher took the chain off Scraggly's neck when she refused to eat. Instead, Sister-in-Law was shut in the wire cage. Sister-in-Law made a fuss but Grandpa ignored her. Grandpa Screecher had begun going in to his shop again, but he returned early and looked downcast. Scraggly refused to go near him. She ate only the bare minimum for survival when he wasn't watching. She roamed outside all day and came home only when she was exhausted. She always returned; she didn't like that about herself.

Today, Scraggly padded into the neighbourhood. She had gone all the way behind the primary school but hadn't found anything. Where had Kori gone? Where did everyone end up? She spotted Grandpa Screecher squatting by the road, his bicycle to the side. She paused in front of the senior citizens' centre. What was he doing? She approached the edge of the road. In the furrows of the field was a long, twisted steel staircase someone had discarded.

'Scraggly, where did you go?' asked Grandpa Screecher.

Scraggly refused to look at him.

'You wander too much,' Grandpa said, sighing. 'I'm the only person who would tolerate a dog like you. Let's go home.'

Scraggly followed slowly, leaving a large gap between them. She stopped in her tracks every time he turned to look at her. Since Kori had been taken by the dog trader, Scraggly shied away whenever he tried to stroke her.

The gate creaked open and they stepped inside. The old cat, who was prowling around the cage, leaped up and ran off. Sister-in-Law began to squawk. 'Let me out! I'll pay you back, you old cat! Do you know what she said to me? She said she couldn't wait to sink her teeth in me!'

Grandpa Screecher ignored the hen and went inside. Scraggly went into her kennel and curled up.

'I'll show her how strong my beak is!' Sister-in-Law grumbled, pacing inside the cage.

Scraggly covered her ears with her paws. She peeked out when she heard the cart rattling. Grandpa Screecher always took his bicycle, unless it was to take the vegetables from the garden to sell. Why was he taking the empty cart out? What was he planning? She tried not to care. She closed her eyes and curled up tighter. She stayed still for a long time, but finally got up and sneaked out under the gate. Grandpa Screecher was nearing the senior citizens' centre. She couldn't see too well, but it looked like he was trying to pull the steel staircase onto the cart. The back of the cart dropped to the ground and the handle was yanked into the air. The wheels moved, and the staircase slid off the cart. Grandpa Screecher almost took a tumble. He tried again, with the same results.

Scraggly squinted and walked forward a few steps. Then she walked closer still. She was approaching the senior citizens' centre now too. Grandpa Screecher placed something behind the wheel to stabilise it and raised one end of the staircase. Someone passing by helped him lift it and secure it onto the cart. Doubled over, he began to pull the cart. The steel staircase was several times longer than the cart, so he moved slowly, dragging the staircase along the ground. Scraggly stayed where she was. Grandpa Screecher's face and neck were glistening with sweat, his lips chapped and his hair covered in dust. 'Move aside,' he ordered.

Scraggly stared up at him.

'Move, I said.'

She stood her ground. If she could speak she would have told him to stop ordering her around. She stared him down. She hadn't planned on doing this, but it felt good.

'Get out of the way!' snapped Grandpa Screecher.

Her fur bristled and she automatically crouched into attack position.

'How dare you!' He began pulling the cart towards her, but she didn't move aside. His heavy footsteps and the cart bore down on her. Scraggly fell over into the creek adjacent to the path. She would have been able to leap over the creek and land on the embankment had she been a little faster, but somehow it felt refreshing to be in the water.

She went home, dripping wet and dirty. Grandpa Screecher

didn't give her a second glance. The staircase was on the ground. He was splayed on the chair like wet washing. He would have stayed that way until dark had a woman not barged in.

'Where's that dog?' she yelled, before Scraggly could even bark.

Grandpa Screecher looked at her, perplexed.

'That dog, didn't she come here?' The woman stabbed the air with her finger.

Scraggly approached slowly, on her guard. Grandpa Screecher's eyes narrowed. 'What?'

'That stupid dog ran away! After biting my husband!'

Grandpa Screecher sat up slowly. Scraggly looked between him and the woman, her head cocked. 'What are you talking about?' Grandpa grumbled. 'What's wrong with you people? Have you never owned a dog before?'

The woman walked around in a huff, looking in the kennel, the wire cage and even the kitchen. 'Where is that dog hiding? Just wait until I catch it.'

Was she talking about Kori? Or was she looking for another dog? How dare this stranger walk in and start mouthing off? Scraggly began barking.

'Shh, Scraggly,' Grandpa said, gesturing. Scraggly grew quiet. 'Where did the dog go?'

'Don't ask me!' shouted the woman. 'It came here.'

'I haven't seen her since your husband took her. It's not my problem even if she did run away,' reasoned Grandpa Screecher.

'She bit him. I need a handful of her fur, at least.'

'Go to the hospital. What use would the fur have?' Grandpa

Screecher got up slowly and opened the wire cage. Sister-in-Law scurried out and climbed the earthenware pots. He opened the door to the kitchen and the shed, and even the front door to the house. 'Take a look. I've sold countless puppies in my lifetime and I've never been treated with such disrespect!'

The woman ignored him and stomped into the house. Just then, the dog trader burst in, a white bandage on his arm. Scraggly lunged at the man, barking. He jumped back, and his wife, having come out to see what the commotion was about, screamed, waving her hands. Scraggly would have gladly bitten him if Grandpa Screecher hadn't grabbed her by the neck.

'Didn't the dog come back here?' demanded the dog trader.

'Are you serious?' Grandpa Screecher tried to drag Scraggly into the wire cage. She dug her feet into the ground. She had to get him this time. But Grandpa Screecher's grip was too strong. Her eyeballs felt as though they would pop out of her sockets. She couldn't even bark.

'Wait. Isn't that your shoe?' asked the woman, pointing at the old shoe hanging on the wire cage.

Scraggly felt dizzy. Grandpa halted in surprise. The dog trader looked uncomfortable. A brief silence came over them.

'Why is that there?' the woman asked.

'What do you mean?' asked the dog trader, faltering.

'Remember, you came home without a shoe a long time ago. Why's it hanging there?' She reached up to take it.

Grandpa Screecher's eyes narrowed. Scraggly's heart somersaulted.

The dog trader yanked back his wife's arm. 'What are you talking about, you silly woman?'

'Look here,' Grandpa Screecher said, his voice shaking with anger. He shut Scraggly in the cage. She watched his trembling hands with anticipation. He plucked the shoe off the cage and held it up. 'Are you sure this is your husband's?' he asked the woman.

'Well ... that's ...' she trailed off, glancing at her husband, who began to fidget.

'I see. So that's it. That's why my dog here has been acting like this every time she sees you.'

'What? What are you talking about? That's not my shoe.' The dog trader shook his head, backing away.

'The thief who stole all our other dogs dropped this shoe. Scraggly here brought it back home. How odd. Your wife says it's yours, but you deny it?'

'Oh, no, no, I must have been mistaken,' the woman said.

The dog trader turned red and his mouth twisted. Grandpa held the old shoe in one hand, looking as though he was about to throw a punch at the dog trader.

'Don't accuse an innocent man!' shouted the dog trader as he backed out of the yard.

'Thieves! Crooks!' thundered Grandpa Screecher, throwing the shoe after them. It hit the dog trader squarely in the back. He ran off without looking round. The woman stood there, dazed, before inching away.

Grandpa Screecher huffed, trying to calm himself down. He

glared at the gate. 'Devious thief,' he grumbled, collapsing into his chair.

That was it. He didn't do anything else. Was that all? Now that he knew who the thief was, couldn't he force him to bring her whole family back? How could he let him run off like that? She banged her head against the wire and growled.

'I knew it!' Grandpa murmured. 'Scraggly, you're quite something.'

Those words soothed the rage that had been roiling inside her. He had always saddened and angered her. He had made her alone in the world. But she was never able to leave him. Why was that? Grandpa Screecher leaned back in his chair. The bright sun made him look transparent, as light as sun-dried linen. Scraggly wasn't sure if she knew him. Perhaps he had always been a stranger. She lay down, her legs stretched out. Her fur dried in stiff peaks, but she didn't shake off the dirt or complain about being shut in the cage.

A short while later, the sun went down. A cool evening breeze began to blow.

'It's Kori! Kori's coming!' Sister-in-Law flapped down from the persimmon tree.

Scraggly raised her head.

'Amazing! She's coming back? A dog who was sold?' shouted the old cat from the top of the wall.

Kori was coming back? Scraggly leaped to her feet and looked at the gate. She couldn't see very well from inside the cage. She saw Grandpa get up slowly, frowning. She placed both paws on the cage and shook it. She could smell her pup, but she smelled strange. Kori squeezed under the gate and approached her, looking bedraggled, her eyes sunken.

'What's wrong, baby?' Scraggly reached out to touch Kori.

Kori eyes were unfocused and her nose was dry. White foam dripped from her mouth. Grandpa Screecher rushed over to examine the pup. Her eyes rolled back and she collapsed.

Scraggly barked.

'What the—?' Grandpa Screecher cradled Kori and pried her mouth open. He peered into her eyes and put his ear to her belly. Scraggly paced while Grandpa took her pup into the kitchen.

'Bring her to me!' Scraggly shook the cage as hard as she could.

'How could this have happened?' clucked Sister-in-Law, pacing between the hallway and the cage. 'This doesn't look good.'

Concerned, the old cat came down to the yard.

'I've seen this before in my hometown. It's really too bad.' Sister-in-Law sighed.

The old cat glanced at Scraggly. 'Kids get hurt,' she said reassuringly. 'That's how they learn and grow up.'

'Let me out!' cried Scraggly.

'But if you come out, I'll be shut in,' reasoned Sister-in-Law.

Scraggly howled. 'Kori! What happened to you?'

'I don't like it in there. I don't want to be shut up again.'

'You stupid hen!' hissed the old cat. 'I wish I could just shut you up!'

'What? What did you say, you stupid feline?' Sister-in-Law gave chase, flapping her wings, and the old cat shot off. The hen ran so energetically that the old cat couldn't make it up the wall; she ran around the yard before she managed to sneak out under the gate.

Grandpa Screecher came out a long time later. 'Come out, Scraggly.'

Scraggly rushed into the kitchen as soon as Grandpa opened the gate. Kori was lying on a blanket. Her breathing was shallow and her chest heaved alarmingly. She smelled of something terrible. She was gurgling. Next to her was a basin of warm water and a long wooden spoon.

'She ate something bad,' Grandpa explained, sighing. 'A poisoned rat or maybe a chicken bone ...' He gently stroked the puppy's heaving belly.

Scraggly looked into her baby's eyes. They were cloudy but she recognised her mother. It was too late to ask what had happened. How was it that they never returned? How was it that when one did, she came back like this?

'Mum ...' Kori let out a thin moan.

Scraggly lowered herself to be closer to her pup. She wanted to take her voice in with her entire being. 'It'll be okay, baby. Don't be afraid.'

Kori's body stiffened. She raised her head. Was she getting better? Reddish-black blood gushed out of her mouth. A terrible smell spread throughout the room. It was as if the sorrow pooled in her body was being released.

Before the blood on the towel dried, before the terrible odour went away, Kori stopped breathing. Scraggly licked her exhausted face and stayed next to her. Grandpa Screecher covered the pup with a blanket and allowed Scraggly some time alone with her baby.

WINDING STAIRCASE

'It wasn't like this at home,' complained Sister-in-Law. 'Nobody looked down on me. How could this be my life?' She plucked at her own feathers pitifully.

'Pluck some more feathers,' suggested the old cat.

'You horrible feline!'

'Careful. You can't get to me.' The old cat placed her paws on the wire cage. Sister-in-Law rushed at her, but the cat moved away.

'Why am I being mistreated like this?' Sister-in-Law looked dejected.

Scraggly didn't pay them any attention. Neither did Grandpa Screecher. For the last two days, Grandpa had been focused on his work in the yard. He was fixing steel, making blue smoke. The welding torch flared. Scraggly flinched and squinted. As soon as the catch on the oxygen tank opened, it hissed. Scraggly marvelled at the blooming flame. Grandpa regulated the red flame into a thin blue one. With it, he cut steel and welded it to another piece of steel. Every time a spark flared against the red metal, the black glass on Grandpa's mask glinted with fire. Sparks landed on his throat and his clothes, burning them with a wisp of white smoke. Scraggly marvelled that flames always left marks behind, even when they died down instantly. Fire turned hard steel soft and malleable. How could Grandpa, who was so thin and weak, do all of this?

'I need a break,' Grandpa Screecher muttered, placing the welding torch down and taking the mask off. His face was shiny with sweat. He sat on his chair. He picked up his glass of water, but glanced at Scraggly. 'I think we have rice wine here somewhere,' he mused. 'There's nothing better when you're parched!' He went inside and came out with a white bottle, filled a cup and drank it down.

Scraggly sniffed at the weld. It was still warm and smelled like metal. It dug deep into her heart, reminding her how much she liked this smell. Grandpa Screecher was making a staircase. A bannister wound around a thick pillar in the middle. He had taken the original rusted steps off and was cutting squares of steel and welding them together to make new ones, carefully putting them on. He looked satisfied, but Scraggly was mystified. Why was he doing this? It was taking so long.

'Come, Scraggly.' Grandpa Screecher poured milky rice wine into her bowl and sat down in his chair.

She cocked her head. It smelled sour. Her nose twitched. She dipped her tongue in the liquid. It was sweet. It wasn't half bad. She lapped it all up.

Grandpa smiled and sat back. 'You know, I feel energised when I see steel. You can make something strong out of it if you know how to use flames. When you put steel together, the welded part can't be more than two millimetres thicker than the steel plate. It won't be smooth, then, you see? You have to make it as if it were always one solid structure. I'm not bad at it, as you can see!'

Scraggly burped.

Grandpa Screecher laughed. 'I can't believe I'm drinking with you. How are you the one keeping me company? My, my.' He closed his eyes.

Scraggly lay down, feeling relaxed.

Sister-in-Law walked around inside her cage, grousing. The old cat crept around the yard. 'Just you wait till I get out of here, just you wait,' Sister-in-Law said, flapping her wings in annoyance. She tried to fly up but hit the ceiling and fell down. She ruffled her feathers.

Grandpa Screecher's head fell on his chest. Both arms dropped under the chair. His white hair danced in the breeze. Scraggly looked at his thin, bare forearm. Her teeth marks were still visible, though the wound had healed. Scraggly gave the scar a gentle lick. The wind grew chilly as the sun set. Grandpa curled up in his sleep. Neither the hen and cat's bickering nor the phone ringing inside woke him up. Would he ever wake up again? All the puppies who had died had been still before they stiffened.

'Grandpa!' shouted a child.

Scraggly got to her feet. Dongi skipped in, Grandma following close behind, a basin balanced on her head. Chanu and his wife came in last.

'Scraggly!' Dongi smiled and held out his arms. She bounded over. He hugged her tightly around the neck. His sweet scent made her feel at peace.

'What are you thinking, staying out here like this when you're not well?' Grandma placed her basin down and woke Grandpa Screecher. He opened his eyes, looking tired, but his face stretched into a smile when he saw Dongi.

The little boy ran over to Grandpa, who got to his feet and picked him up. 'You've come home so early!'

'Happy birthday!' Dongi cried.

Grandpa Screecher danced around with Dongi in his arms. 'My birthday is tomorrow, but it can be any day as long as you're here celebrating with me!' He spun around. Scraggly scampered after them, feeling more at ease around the little boy.

'Father, we're here!' It was Chanu's sister and her family. Their daughter Yeoni ran up. Grandpa Screecher held Dongi in one arm and picked up his granddaughter with the other. He continued to dance.

'What are you doing with this?' Chanu pointed at the steel staircase.

Grandpa Screecher put the children down and picked up his hammer. He tapped it against the welded areas to check that they were properly fused. 'Good. Now, help me a little.'

Chanu dug a hole under the persimmon tree and the son-in-law gathered the tools strewn in the yard.

Dongi came over and straddled the staircase. 'What's this, Grandpa?'

'It's a staircase. A snail staircase!'

'A snail?'

'Right.' Grandpa Screecher pointed. 'The inside of a snail's shell goes round and round like this.'

'Oh, so it's a staircase for snails!'

Grandpa Screecher laughed. 'It's for you, Dongi! And for you, Yeoni. It's for you to go up carefully and slowly, just like a snail. I made this so you can go to the top of the tree. When the persimmons are ripe, you can go up and pick them yourselves.'

'You can just pick them for us,' suggested Dongi.

'That's true. But . . . '

'But what?'

'If I'm not here, I can't pick them for you. So you'll have to pick them.'

'Why won't you be here? You're right here!' Dongi tapped Grandpa Screecher's chest and giggled.

Everyone paused silently before returning to their work. Chanu dug the hole, the son-in-law put tools away in the shed, Grandma washed the vegetables at the well, and the women went into the kitchen.

Scraggly snuck off.

'Damn. Betrayal is excruciating,' spat the old cat from under the wall.

'That's a strange way of putting it,' Scraggly said. 'I don't know what you're talking about.'

'It means you can't trust anyone in this world.'

Scraggly glanced at the old cat. She knew what that felt like.

The old cat rubbed her eyes and nose. 'Do I look very old?'

Scraggly didn't answer.

'I mean, my eyes are failing. And my sense of smell is weak.'

'What's wrong with getting older?' Scraggly asked.

'That's precisely what I mean,' the cat said grouchily. 'What's wrong with getting old? I've lived ten years with my owner, but she brought home a brand new cat. Do you know what that feels like?'

Scraggly felt bad for the old cat. If it hadn't been for her nauseating odour, she might even have forgotten that she was a cat.

'I'm going to drive it out. It's taking my place.' The old cat turned around, but her shoulders drooped and her tail dragged on the floor.

The men were raising the staircase.

'Be careful,' Chanu said. 'Hold it tight.'

'I've got it. Pour cement in the hole,' ordered Grandpa.

'It looks great! You should paint it – maybe blue,' suggested the son-in-law.

Scraggly looked up at Grandpa Screecher's work being raised next to the tree. The steel staircase wound around the persimmon tree. Climbing the stairs one at a time, you could circle the large tree once, and reach the top of the tree on the tenth step. The staircase looked like it was either protecting the tree or leaning against it. The gentle curves somehow resembled Grandpa Screecher, who was standing hunched over, looking at his staircase.

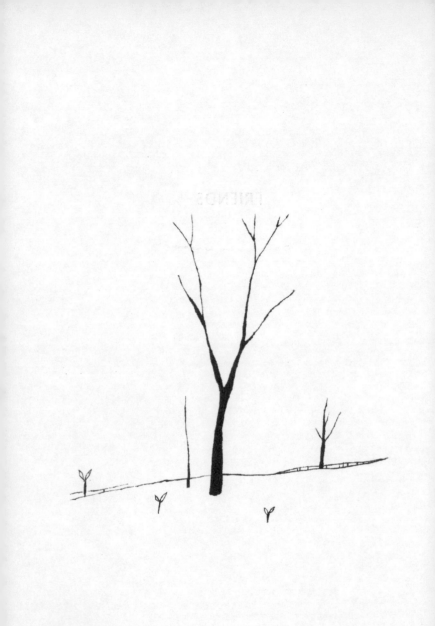

FRIENDS

'**G**et out right now!' Scraggly scolded.

Sister-in-Law ignored her, as she always did. She seemed to think that she could do anything she wanted. She pecked the cabbage in the vegetable patch, leaped up onto the earthenware pots, and ate the fish lying out to dry. According to the old cat, she even went next door to steal the new kitten's food.

'You're such a headache!' Scraggly grumbled.

'You're the headache! Why can't you stop bothering me? I can't even rest peacefully!' yelled the hen as she fluttered up to the persimmon tree. She was getting chubbier by the day but she still could fly with vigour.

The old cat leaped from wall to roof to avoid her. 'Just you wait. As soon as I have the chance . . .'

Sister-in-Law sniggered. 'All you do is yap. You think I'm scared of you? Prove that you're not a scaredy-cat. Instead of running away, why don't you come over here?' She puffed her chest out and went menacingly towards the wall.

The old cat retreated and disappeared.

Scraggly sighed and went into her kennel. Where was Grandpa Screecher? She forced down the cold, dry food in her bowl even though she didn't have any appetite. Grandma had poured it at dawn. The hen would take it if she didn't eat it, and this might be all there was for the day. She hadn't even seen Grandpa Screecher for a few days. Only Grandma, who left early and returned home late at night. It was too quiet. Scraggly stretched and shivered, and came back outside.

The old cat slid down the drainpipe. 'Are you going to the bus stop again? It's no use, you know.'

Scraggly walked by without answering and passed under the gate. The old cat smacked her lips and ambled behind her, along the embankment. She had become thin since the kitten arrived; now she hung around outside most of the time. Scraggly stood at the bus stop and watched the cars pass by. Some cars kept going and others stopped, but Grandpa Screecher didn't come. It had been the same yesterday and the day before that. She would give up and go home, and Grandma would eventually come home, turn on the lights, and feed her.

The streetlights came on. It was time to go back. Sometimes, waiting for Grandpa felt like she was waiting for her mother and siblings and her puppies all over again. No matter how long she waited, he never came. Scraggly padded back towards home, along the wall. The old cat ran up to her, panting, smelling horrible as usual. Scraggly stopped in her tracks.

'Guess what I found out?' asked the cat.

Scraggly frowned, annoyed at the cat's penchant for talking in riddles. It would be easier if she got to the point right away, since she was going to have to explain what she meant eventually.

'Guess what you can do for me?' said the old cat, grinning.

Scraggly glared at her.

The old cat tried again. 'Scraggly, what will you do for me if I tell you something important?'

'What do you want?'

'Hm. Well ... you don't have anything of value ...'

'Stop, I'm tired of your games.'

'Oh, I know. You can be my friend. A friend who won't betray me. A real friend.'

'But I'm a dog. And you're a cat.'

'That's what makes it even more special.'

'I'm off,' Scraggly said, fed up. 'I can't leave the house empty.'

'Oh, it's fine. That chatterbox hen is there. I'm going to get her soon, you know. My owner is so upset because she keeps pecking our cute kitten.'

Scraggly snorted and began walking home.

'Hey, where are you going? You didn't say you'll be my friend.'

'Why would I want to?'

'Well, let's see. Why should you?'

'This is silly.' Scraggly shook her head.

The old cat grinned and blocked her way. 'Oh, I remember now! The white one.'

'What are you talking about?'

'Your baby, the white one. I figured out where he lives. Aren't you curious to see how he grew up?'

Scraggly stared into the old cat's eyes. She had never believed her before. Could she now? The cat's large, twinkling eyes invited her trust. 'My baby?'

'I know where he lives. That's what I'm saying.'

Scraggly stepped towards her, and the old cat leaped back. They were a dog and a cat, after all.

'He must have got some education,' the old cat said, after she'd recovered herself. 'He's really important. He's become famous. Everyone knows about him!'

'Where does he live?'

'Not far. You know the nursery school behind the church? Behind that is the tofu factory, and to the left of that is the mill. You know, once you pass the mill, there's a school. You know, where kids go. Behind that . . .' The cat tailed off.

'Good grief! And? So where behind that?'

'Well, you know – I don't actually know,' confessed the cat.

'What? Are you winding me up?'

'No, no. I heard from a cat I know who lives in a musician's house somewhere behind the school. The owner plays some kind of instrument, I gather.'

'Wait. What does this have to do with my puppy? I can't believe I'm listening to you. This is pathetic.' Scraggly shoved the old cat aside.

The old cat bristled. 'That's where the puppy lives! In the cat's house!'

'He lives there?'

'According to my source, yes.'

'Oh!' Scraggly smiled and turned to face the old cat, who grinned back.

Scraggly began to gallop, flying down the alley. It was getting dark but she wasn't worried. The house would be fine. Would he recognise her? He must be so big by now. Scraggly imagined wonderful things. She tried to follow the cat's instructions but she wasn't entirely sure where to go. She had gone around the school before, but the problem was after that. She couldn't begin to guess where the musician lived. It was so dark that she couldn't see anything. And she had left the house empty. She would have to return tomorrow, during the day. Scraggly turned around regretfully, looking back again and again. She floated home. She vowed to do whatever the old cat wanted next time she saw her. Sure, it was a little odd to have a cat as a friend, but she could easily rile Sister-in-Law to please her new buddy.

Was nobody home? Scraggly tensed as she walked up to the gates. Grandma should have been home by now, but the windows were dark and the house was still. Her hair stood on end. It didn't feel right. What was that unpleasant smell?

'Why is it so quiet?' she called. 'Hey, Sister-in-Law!'

No answer.

'Stop joking around and come out!' Scraggly stood in the middle of the yard, looking around. She squinted and pricked up her ears. She heard something coming from the pumpkin vine by the wall. She ran over. The closer she went, the stronger the smell became.

'Scraggly . . .'

It was the old cat, nearing death. Next to her was Sister-in-Law, already stiff.

'Damn it,' moaned the old cat. 'She got me.'

'Wake up!' Scraggly stamped her feet, but she could tell it was too late.

'Don't tell anyone that I was done in by a hen, okay?' The old cat's breaths grew ragged.

Scraggly nodded. 'Stay strong.' She licked the old cat's wounds.

The old cat blinked, trying to keep her eyes open. 'Hey, look . . . you're glowing again. I told you you're different.'

'It's your eyes playing tricks, I'm sure.'

'No, the darker it gets the better I can see you.'

Scraggly glanced down at her front paws. Her fur did look different. Was it the old cat's words, or the moonlight? The cat stopped trembling.

'Hey!' She shook the cat, but the cat didn't open her eyes again. Scraggly sat still for a long time, dazed. To her, the old cat had always been an annoying, hateful neighbour, never a friend. But she had known her for a long time. And tomorrow, she wouldn't be perched there on the wall any more. Her eyes welled up. She was completely alone. She picked up the still-soft body of the cat with her mouth and went next door. She knew the old cat would want to be home, even in death.

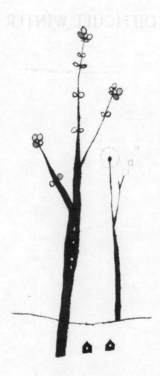

DIFFICULT WINTER

Caw, caw, caw.

Scraggly opened her eyes and looked out. Her body ached from being curled up in the cold. A magpie was grooming its feathers on the frost-covered persimmon tree. The few fruit hanging from the top were unusually red. The windows were still closed. Nobody had come home yesterday. Her bowl seemed emptier and colder than usual. Scraggly went to the pumpkin vine, remembering that Sister-in-Law remained under the frozen leaves. Her body was unmarked. The old cat must have finished her off quickly. She looked as though she were merely sleeping under a blanket of frost. Scraggly looked up at the wall, which was shiny with frost too. No cat. So last night hadn't been a dream.

Scraggly left the vegetable garden. All the cabbage had frozen. If Grandpa Screecher had been there, he wouldn't have left any cabbage in the fields. Not only that, the yard wouldn't be piled with leaves, the shed door wouldn't be open and rattling, and the tap would be tightly closed rather than leaking all day. She wouldn't be starving. Scraggly stretched out. Her breath formed white puffs and disappeared. There was something she had to do, even though she was cold and hungry. Would she recognise him? She left the house and retraced her steps from the night before. But she got lost again behind the school. Where could the musician's house be? What was a musician, anyway?

She would wait all day long if she had to. If he had grown into a dog everyone knew, she would be able to recognise him too. After all, he was her baby. Scraggly walked up and down the streets to keep warm. She walked down all the roads around the school. Since her baby might be going another way while she was on a different path, she looked all around her as she moved about. She didn't have time to dwell on how cold and hungry she was. She stopped in front of the flower shop, thunderstruck. There he was. The white dog. He was large, with straight ears and long legs. But she realised that the dog she was staring at had longer fur than the white dog. And he had a tint of brown to his white fur. Scraggly smiled. Here he was, looking so much like his father. She couldn't call him baby, though; he was all grown up. Her heart pounded. She gazed meaningfully at him as he walked towards her. She understood now what the old cat had meant; he was leading his master – a man who couldn't see – with a confident expression, wearing a leather leash. 'Little one ...' she said in a tiny voice, not wanting to distract him.

He passed by without hearing her. She didn't mind. Her heart was full as she watched him walk on, his footsteps light and his tail wagging pleasantly. The old cat had been a true friend. Until now, she had believed that all of her babies had met a terrible fate, but she realised that she'd been proved wrong. Here was one of her pups, grown up and dignified.

Scraggly followed at a distance until she got to the three-way road in front of Grandpa Screecher's junk shop. Her pup turned down a street she had never taken. She stopped. Grandpa's shuttered shop reminded her of her empty house, and she knew she wasn't young enough to wander into unfamiliar territory.

'Goodbye, little one.' Scraggly nodded at her pup, who walked along merrily. She turned and didn't look back.

When she reached the corner at the National Agricultural Cooperative, Scraggly spotted Chanu's car. He was unloading it. That meant Grandpa Screecher would already be home. Scraggly bounded into the alley towards the house. She could smell his scent but couldn't see him. Then she spotted him in the dry creek bed, moaning. He must have slipped and fallen.

Barking, Scraggly tumbled down to the creek bed and curled around Grandpa Screecher. He was shivering, his forehead bloodied. She barked intently, hoping Chanu would hear her.

'Scraggly ...' Grandpa Screecher tugged at her weakly. She grew scared when she felt his cold fingers.

'Oh, my goodness!' Grandma ran up, hurrying down into the creek bed. 'I'm so sorry!'

'Oww ...'

'I went ahead to get the house warm. I thought Chanu was following!'

Grandpa Screecher moaned. Chanu ran to help his father up. He heaved him onto his back. Scraggly followed close behind, staring at the old man's arms and legs swinging limply. She stayed outside as everyone else bustled into the house. The cold arid wind swept leaves around the yard.

A few days later, the house was empty once again. Grandpa Screecher had been taken to the hospital early in the morning. Yeongseon came by later that night to take some things to the hospital, and after that nobody came back. Scraggly had been given a lump of cold, hard rice. She didn't have any water. She was afraid.

Caw, caw, caw, the magpie cried, pecking at the sole persimmon remaining at the top of the tree. If the bird stopped coming, Scraggly would truly be alone. She missed having the old cat around, even when she had come by just to jeer. She missed Sister-in-Law too. Even the annoying hen was better than being alone. She wished she could fall asleep. Her empty stomach made her feel even colder, though she was curled up. If the cage were open Scraggly would go inside; at least there was a blanket in there. The kennel was so cold.

'Anyone home?' The acupuncturist stepped in.

Scraggly licked her chops and poked her head out, smelling food.

The woman tried the front door, but finding it locked, turned to face Scraggly. 'Poor thing, suffering along with your owner.' Frowning, she poured the food into Scraggly's bowl. She hoped for broth, but it was kimchi pancakes. She wolfed it down anyway.

'I wonder if the surgery went well,' the woman muttered before leaving.

Scraggly's throat closed up. Grandpa Screecher must be very ill. She shivered. She had to eat something else. Her innards felt

160

twisted from hunger. She padded slowly out of the gate. Her knees ached. She walked around the fields, steadying her shaking legs. Snow had fallen overnight and it felt even colder out here. There was nothing to eat anywhere. She went to the acupuncturist's. She'd gratefully take anything, even more kimchi pancakes.

The acupuncturist's dog growled and bared his teeth. He had got big and his face looked stubborn. He looked vastly different from the little yappy dog who had come by hoping to chat and be friends. 'You're a nobody now,' the dog jeered.

Scraggly felt her face flush. She wanted to turn around but her body wouldn't listen. The bowl in front of the dog was overflowing with steaming food. She wanted to eat so badly that tears sprang to her eyes. Without thinking twice, she rushed forward and took a bite.

'What do you think you're doing?' the dog yelled, biting her on the shoulder. His sharp teeth tore into her flesh. But she managed to swallow what was in her mouth. She reached out for more but he was still gripping her shoulder; he shook it wildly. She fell down. She wanted to cry.

'A dog follows the fate of her owner,' the dog warned. 'I hear the old man is on the verge of death. Don't you realise you're behaving shamefully?'

She should leave. The food she had swallowed stuck in her throat. She shivered. The cold wind stabbed at her open wound.

Back home, she hesitated in front of her kennel. She didn't want to go inside, but there was nowhere else for her to go. They'd be home soon, when she woke up. She went in and curled up. The cold chilled her bones, and she curled up tighter.

THE ROAD TO FRIENDSHIP

'What happened to you?'

Scraggly opened her eyes. Grandpa Screecher's wrinkly face was nearby. She wanted to lick him but her mouth was full of food. He was spooning gruel into her mouth.

'This won't do ...' The lines on his face grew deeper when Scraggly threw it all up. His bony hand caressed her neck, belly and legs. But his hand didn't feel warm or gentle; she couldn't feel anything.

'I'll do it,' Grandma said, taking the spoon. 'You go in and rest.'

Grandpa Screecher pulled himself up, holding onto the wall. He and Scraggly looked at each other. He had grown thin and much older. His cheekbones were protruding. 'Eat, eat. So you can live. At the very least, you should live.' His eyes were sunken, so deep and transparent that it seemed as though he were looking elsewhere.

Scraggly looked around. It was warm. She was in the kitchen.

'Here, eat,' Grandma said, spooning gruel into her mouth. 'You need to live so your master feels hopeful.'

Scraggly wanted to eat it, but she couldn't swallow. Something hard was lodged in her chest. She vomited again. Grandma sighed and stopped trying. Scraggly felt dizzy. She closed her eyes. It wasn't cold any more, and Grandpa Screecher was back. She wanted everything to stay just like this. She fell asleep again. When she woke she was still so dizzy that she couldn't open her eyes. From time to time, though her eyes were shut, Scraggly heard what was going on around her. Grandma was bustling about. Grandpa Screecher was moaning. It all sounded as though it was coming from far away.

'I'm sorry, but I can't let him see you like this. It will bring bad luck.' Grandma struggled to pick Scraggly up. She was placed outside; Grandma stroked her for a moment. It was chilly, yet she felt neither cold nor sad. The wind that was blowing through her heart felt nice and cool. She kept dozing. Even when she was awake, she didn't open her eyes. It suddenly occurred to her that she needed to get up. She had to get to her kennel. She stood slowly. Her body was stiff. Of course, she hadn't eaten anything. And she hadn't moved for a long time. But something was different. One of her back legs wouldn't move. She couldn't walk properly because of the curled leg. Scraggly toppled over and stayed like that for a long time. Finally, she got up and stumbled along. She fell a few times but managed to make it to the kennel.

She would feel better after she got some more sleep. She lay down in the most comfortable position she could find. She closed her eyes again. From far away, she heard music. Her heart swelled.

Sobs burst from the house. She could hear people rushing around, crying. Scraggly tried to open her eyes to see what was happening, but her eyelids were so heavy. They were glued together. They wouldn't budge. There was a moment of peace; everything stopped. She should open her eyes and get up.

'Scraggly?' It was Grandpa Screecher.

She raised her head. She felt light. He sounded so upbeat, infusing her with energy. The sun was so bright when she finally opened her eyes. She soon became used to the glow. The persimmon tree was thick with leaves. The flower patch overflowed with blooms.

'Scraggly?' Grandpa Screecher called again.

She blinked. The voice was coming from the tree. Or rather, from the snail staircase. The persimmon tree was standing tall against the sky. When had it grown that tall? The stairs were covered by green branches and stretched up endlessly.

Grandpa was climbing the steps, beckoning to her. Behind him scampered pups; her spotted sibling who had died in the garden and the weak black pup, her very first. Scraggly smiled and bounded over. Puppies who'd hardly had the chance to walk were now climbing the stairs, and her old friend was calling her.